"Look out!" Eloise shouted.

She had the widest grin Blake had ever seen as she plummeted toward him, sliding down the banister a thousand miles an hour, totally out of control.

Flying off the end, she smashed into him, driving the air from his lungs as she landed squarely on his chest.

"Whee! I've never done that before and I've always wanted to." Her blue eyes sparkled as if she'd kidnapped a skyful of fireworks. "I tried once at the British Museum, but the guard stopped me."

Didn't this woman know how to behave at a business meeting? Blake coughed and sucked in a ragged breath. "Have you ever considered showing a little restraint?"

"Not me. Life is too short."

"Then maybe you'd at least think about getting off me." Then again, maybe it was time *he* did something foolish...like forget his strictly-business code and kiss her senseless....

S0-AGF-627

Dear Reader,

Valentine's brings more wonderful and funny books from LOVE & LAUGHTER!

Courting Cupid, by popular Harlequin American Romance author Charlotte Maclay, wonders what happens when Cupid notches her bow, takes careful aim...and misses, bringing together the most unlikely couple! You'll laugh out loud at the antics of the gang on the corporate retreat and sigh as Eloise and Blake fall in love.

Then, in *Send Me No Flowers,* Kristin Gabriel takes her revenge for all of us who sometimes get a little fed up with all the hoopla surrounding Valentine's Day. This fast-paced comedy pits a sexy mayor against a determined therapist. While both Drew and Rachel have good arguments for opposing or supporting the Valentine's Day festival, it is their hearts that win the battle. I hope you enjoy this story as much as I did.

Have a happy Valentine's Day!

Malle Vallik

Malle Vallik
Associate Senior Editor

COURTING CUPID
Charlotte Maclay

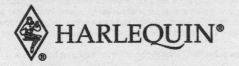

HARLEQUIN®

TORONTO • NEW YORK • LONDON
AMSTERDAM • PARIS • SYDNEY • HAMBURG
STOCKHOLM • ATHENS • TOKYO • MILAN • MADRID
PRAGUE • WARSAW • BUDAPEST • AUCKLAND

ISBN 0-373-44061-8

COURTING CUPID

Copyright © 1999 by Charlotte Lobb

All rights reserved. Except for use in any review, the reproduction or utilization of this work in whole or in part in any form by any electronic, mechanical or other means, now known or hereafter invented, including xerography, photocopying and recording, or in any information storage or retrieval system, is forbidden without the written permission of the publisher, Harlequin Enterprises Limited, 225 Duncan Mill Road, Don Mills, Ontario, Canada M3B 3K9.

All characters in this book have no existence outside the imagination of the author and have no relation whatsoever to anyone bearing the same name or names. They are not even distantly inspired by any individual known or unknown to the author, and all incidents are pure invention.

This edition published by arrangement with Harlequin Books S.A.

® and TM are trademarks of the publisher. Trademarks indicated with ® are registered in the United States Patent and Trademark Office, the Canadian Trade Marks Office and in other countries.

Printed in U.S.A.

A funny thing happened...

I spend a lot of time in front of my computer, and I really get tired of telemarketers phoning and interrupting my thoughts, especially when I'm deep in the middle of writing a really great scene. The other day, interrupted once again, I finally got up the nerve to do what I've always longed to do. Before the caller got started on his spiel, I asked in my sexiest voice, "What are you wearing?" "A shirt," he replied, puzzled. I inquired about the color. "Uh, brown." And if he was wearing a tie, would he loosen it? "Uh, okay." Still not giving away I was pulling a practical joke on the poor, confused man, I requested that he undo the top button of his shirt. That's when I heard the click.

I much prefer to hear from my readers. You can reach me at P.O. Box 505, Torrance, CA 90508

—Charlotte Maclay

Books by Charlotte Maclay

HARLEQUIN LOVE & LAUGHTER
 29—ACCIDENTAL ROOMMATES

HARLEQUIN AMERICAN ROMANCE
620—THE BEWITCHING BACHELOR
643—WANTED: A DAD TO BRAG ABOUT
657—THE LITTLEST ANGEL
684—STEALING SAMANTHA
709—CATCHING A DADDY
728—A LITTLE BIT PREGNANT

Don't miss any of our special offers. Write to us at the following address for information on our newest releases.

Harlequin Reader Service
U.S.: 3010 Walden Ave., P.O. Box 1325, Buffalo, NY 14269
Canadian: P.O. Box 609, Fort Erie, Ont. L2A 5X3

1

"WERE IT NOT for affirmative action, my dear, we would not be having this discussion."

Eloise winced at Hubert's condescending tone. The section chief for Cupid's Celestial Division had a decidedly sexist attitude about employing only males in his department.

"I received this notice of reassignment," Eloise explained for the second time, moving forward to place the form on Hubert's glittering gold-filigreed desk. Tiny tufts of iridescent clouds drifted out of the way. "I'm quite sure I'll be able to handle whatever job you give me."

"No doubt with the same competence you've demonstrated as a guardian angel," he said. One corner of his Cupid's bow mouth curled with disdain.

He *would* have to bring that up, Eloise thought with a sigh. "Circumstances have tended to conspire against me, sir. I'm sure if they had given me another chance—"

"Your record with the Baby Division was just as dismal."

Her shoulders slumped. "I was simply trying to

show a little initiative on the job. That baby had been waiting for so long—''

"Ms. Periwinkle." He cut her off sharply.

Standing, he marched around his desk to stand in front of her. He wasn't much taller upright, nor any more physically imposing, than he had been seated, Eloise noted. She could still see the top of his shiny domed head, and she wasn't a particularly tall angel. She was also among the lowest ranked angels, currently without portfolio. Which meant she had to go wherever she was assigned. And there weren't that many divisions left where she hadn't already tried—and failed.

"I don't believe you fully appreciate, Ms. Periwinkle, the difficulties and challenges of being an apprentice cupid. The task is not for the faint of heart. Bungling an assignment can lead to disastrous consequences, events that may affect earth and its people for centuries."

"It doesn't seem all that hard to get a man and woman to fall in love," she said with a determined shake of her head that set her blond curls bouncing. In fact, she thought it would be a wonderful job to have. Quite uplifting.

Hubert's eyes widened, making them as round as his cherubic face. He wore a white shirt with a mandarin collar and white pants, neither of which had so much as a smudge on them. In contrast, Eloise's white robe always looked dingy gray and frequently suffered from her calamitous forays to earth.

"Evidently you have not heard of Napoleon and Josephine," Hubert said.

"Well, I've heard..."

"Our worst disaster, I'm afraid. Young Napoleon was supposed to fall in love with that sweet Evette. Charming girl, she was. But a sudden breeze caught the arrow and it went astray. Poof!" He snapped his stubby thumb and middle finger together. "Instead of living a quiet life as a country gentleman, Napoleon went on a rampage to please that Josephine by acquiring *more* land, *more* wealth. The woman simply would *not* be satisfied until he'd conquered everything in sight."

"I hadn't realized," Eloise admitted.

"Yes, and then there was Edward the Eighth. Abdicating his throne for that Simpson woman! What nonsense."

"I thought it was sweet."

Cherubs were not supposed to scowl. Hubert did.

"I don't imagine you even know how to shoot a bow and arrow."

"I'm sure I can learn." How hard could it be? Little boys managed it all the time. Certainly a full-grown woman could figure it out, given a chance to practice.

"That is yet to be proven, my dear." From the corner of his desk Hubert picked up two file folders. "These are your targets. I suggest you study the information carefully. You'll note Blake Donovan and Margaret Wykowski live in vastly different parts of their country. They'll be together for only four days at a corporate retreat. If you don't manage to get them to fall in love during that time, it is doubtful they will manage it on their own by telepathy, don't you agree?''

"Oh, yes, sir. I understand that." Standing a little straighter, she accepted the files. *Her very first Cupid assignment.* She was bursting with pride.

Hubert dismissed her with a wave of his hand, then turned back to his desk.

Not quite sure of the proper protocol, Eloise backed out of the room.

Once outside, she found a quiet spot away from the hub of activity and settled on a gilded bench to read through the files. She could hear the harp choir practicing in the distance. Such lovely music. She really wished she were a more skilled musician.... But being a cupid was equally as important, she told herself, opening the first folder.

Blake Donovan, she discovered, had not had an easy life. Raised without a father, he'd taken over much of that responsibility for himself, helping his mother and caring for his younger sister from quite a young age. And he was still looking after them.

"Oh, the sweet man," she murmured, admiring someone with that much heart. "He's worked so hard all his life, he deserves to find love." She flipped to the next page in the file and cocked a brow at the notation regarding Blake's future offspring. "Will you look at that!" Blake's son would grow up to be an outstanding astronomer who would lead a crucial exploration of the galaxy.

"No wonder Hubert thought this assignment was so critical," Eloise said as she calculated earth years. "If Blake doesn't begin his own family soon, his son won't be born in time to carry out the space mission."

Redoubling her resolve to not fail, Eloise checked Margaret Wykowski's file. Yes, she could see right away that the two of them would make a perfect couple. Margaret was both hardworking and brilliant. Only once in her entire life had she received anything less than an A grade. And that single B had resulted in Margaret's being grounded for a month.

Eloise frowned. That seemed a harsh punishment for an eleven-year-old girl who should have been out having some fun with her friends.

"Thank goodness I didn't have to report to Margaret's parents whenever I messed up," Eloise muttered with a wry grin. She never would have gotten off the harp cleaning detail.

She scanned the rest of the file, becoming increasingly confident that Blake Donovan and Margaret Wykowski were meant for each other. Why, Eloise concluded, it was entirely likely that even if the Cupid Division didn't intervene, these two would fall in love anyway.

At last Eloise had been given an assignment she was sure she could handle.

Well, *almost* sure, she conceded, recalling her prior calamities. But this time...

STRIDING INTO his office, Blake Donovan threw an order at his secretary. "Bring me the file on Snappy Pizza."

"In a minute, sugar," she drawled. "My fingernails are drying."

Blake gritted his teeth. He'd spent years perfecting his don't-mess-with-me image, a by-product of his misspent youth. But for some reason, Paula Nicklesworth had never bought into the act.

"Just how long do you think it will take for your nails to be sufficiently dry so you can do a little work around here?" He leveled her what he thought was his most intimidating look.

She didn't so much as flutter an eyelash. "Fifteen or twenty minutes, I'd say. I've got a heavy date tonight and you wouldn't want me to have chipped nails, would you?"

"Heaven forbid," he muttered.

Long, lanky and loose-limbed, Paula continued to blow on her fingernails; she rarely moved at a speed faster than dead slow, in spite of his intimidations.

When she'd first applied for the job, he had to admit he'd considered bedding her. But knowing that qualified secretaries were a damned sight harder to find than rolls in the hay, he had long since resolved to never mix business and pleasure.

And almost to his surprise, he had gotten far more than a nickel's worth of work out of Paula. As the southeastern regional marketing manager of Crest Enterprises—the largest manufacturer of electronic signs and billboards in the country—he was secretly pleased with his decision to hire her.

"So show me where the damn file is and I'll get it myself," he said, moving across the room.

Having won yet another skirmish, Paula smirked at him with her glossy red lips. "Sure thing, sugar." She stood and sashayed across the room to stand in front of a row of puke-yellow filing cabinets.

"Did you confirm with Crankshank that the management retreat is still on for tomorrow?" he asked.

One long fire-engine-red fingernail tapped delicately on the middle drawer. "He called to remind you that the last ferry to the island departs at five o'clock. You miss it and you'll miss the opening ceremonies."

"I'll be there." Leaning across Paula to get to the filing cabinet, Blake resisted asking why Snappy Pizza was filed under "H-to-L." Her answers to his questions always sounded so logical. But left on his own, he couldn't seem to re-create the thought processes that had made her system seem so simple.

In his experience, women were like that—convoluted.

Fortunately for him, he had no intention of complicating his life any further by getting emotionally involved with any woman. Temporary relationships were just fine by him. He had more than enough responsibilities with his own family.

"Mr. Crankshank also mentioned that Harry Poliste will be retiring soon and won't be attending the retreat," Paula said between puffs of air as she blew on her fingernails. "Crankshank will be making the decision about who will replace Poliste while you're all there.''

Blake's head snapped up and he almost broke his neck whipping it around to look at Paula. "You mean he's going to decide who gets the vice president of Marketing job based on how well we perform at this retreat?"

Her shoulders rose in a slow shrug. "It sounds like that's what he has in mind."

Blake swore under his breath. Obadiah Crankshank, the company president, had been known to base major corporate decisions on nothing more than a whim. And the annual management retreat, a screwy combination of motivational hype and treasure hunt, was rife with whimsy as far as Blake was concerned. A testament to Crankshank's piratical ancestor who had first settled Crankshank Island and supposedly buried a chestful of gold doubloons, the retreat was Crankshank's means to an end. To find the gold. To relive the story—if the old stories were to be believed. Which Blake didn't.

But he could taste being vice president of Marketing—number two man in the whole damn company— as clearly as he could recall the flavor of sweet cream poured over fresh Georgia peaches.

Man, did he want that job! He deserved it, too.

No other region had the sales his group had racked up. His performance was head and shoulders above that of any other regional director—Margaret Wykowski, standout from the western region included. Which didn't mean squat if Obadiah Crankshank got it into his head to promote someone because of a quirky fluke that happened in a child's game.

Whatever the rules for this year's treasure hunt, Blake vowed he'd win. Never before had there been so much riding on the outcome. For a kid from the wrong side of the tracks, being named vice president at the ripe old age of thirty-two would be like snatching the gold ring.

He carried the Snappy Pizza file into his office, savoring the possibilities. *Vice President Donovan* had a nice ring to it. Not that Paula would be impressed. But his nephew Stevie might be.

Outside his office window, the late afternoon sun glistened off the Atlanta skyline. Stevie had Little League practice that afternoon and had asked Blake to help out with the coaching. Maybe he could still get there in time to help the kids with their batting practice.

But first, Snappy Pizza. He'd read in the *Wall Street Journal* that the franchise was expanding into his territory and had opened a regional office. They'd need new signs. He intended Crest Enterprises to be the supplier.

For him, the company motto—With The Right Sign You Can Reach The World—had become a mantra. So far it had been a damned lucrative philosophy.

Blake glanced at the clock when Paula buzzed him, announcing his sister was on the line. Four o'clock and he'd forgotten all about Stevie's game.

"Hey, Caroline, I'm really sorry—"

"Blake. It's…" Her voice caught. "It's Stevie. There's been an accident."

Blake's stomach clenched. "How bad?"

"He's all right," she hastened to say. "I'm mean, he's not dead or anything that awful. He broke his ankle jumping off the bleachers. I'm sorry to bother you, honest I am."

"It's okay, sis." The tension that had gripped him eased by a fraction to be replaced by a sense of guilt that he might have prevented the accident if he'd been there. But all kids broke bones now and again. It wasn't the end of the world.

"The problem is the hospital, Blake. Stevie's going to need surgery and then months of therapy. They want me…" She sobbed a little on the other end of the line.

Blake knew what the hospital wanted. Money. Paid right up front. And his sister's part-time job didn't include much in the way of fringe benefits let alone a dime's worth of insurance.

"Don't worry, sis. I'll cover the cost of whatever needs to be done."

"I never meant to be a burden to you."

"Hey, what's a big brother for?" He spun around in his chair and glanced out the window at the sky-line. A medical bill like this one would likely be a doozie. He was already picking up a big part of the tab for his mother's care.

"They want you to sign something, Blake, before they take him into surgery."

"Right. Tell 'em I'll be there in a half hour."

As he hung up the phone, Blake concluded the stakes for the sales director's retreat had just gone up a notch. A big bonus went along with the promotion to vice president. Blake needed that extra money.

Stevie was a terrific kid and his future would depend upon it.

THE ARROW MISSED the mark by a celestial mile.

Eloise sighed. You'd think a magic dart so small it couldn't be seen by the human eye would track a little better.

"Don't worry about it, sweetheart." Her archery instructor sat cross-legged on a pillow of clouds behind her. "You're never going to make the grade anyway."

She frowned at him. "I can do this. Just give me a little more time to—"

"It won't do you any good. They're gonna give you the hardest case they can find. Even hitting the bull's-eye won't budge whoever they give you when it comes to love. So you might as well give up."

"I never give up," Eloise said stoutly, raising her chin a notch. She got fired or reassigned fairly often, she admitted, but she never gave up.

Like the time she'd been in the Prayer Answering Department. A sweet little boy had been wishing for a puppy so hard she heard his voice over the tumult of other requests. Unfortunately, he lived in the projects and couldn't have a pet. So she'd first had to find a decent job for his father, and help the family to save enough money to buy a cute little place in the suburbs with a fenced yard. Of course, by then the youngster had been twenty-five years old, had a college degree and already moved away from home. Her superiors suggested she'd spent just a wee bit too much time and effort on one case; they reassigned her elsewhere. It hadn't mattered that the boy's family had loved the stray mixed-poodle-and-Dalmatian puppy she'd sent them.

"Besides," she said to her archery instructor, "I've read the files. My targets are perfectly suited for each other."

"Don't count on it." He shook his head. "Being a cupid is a guy thing, Eloise. We don't want women messing with our stuff. If you succeed, other females will want to try it, and the next thing you know, the whole universe will be believing in all that mushy love business."

"But you're a senior cupid," she protested, appalled by his cynicism. "You must believe—"

"Hey, I've got myself a posh job here, sweetheart. I don't want the likes of you messing with it. And as soon as you blow your assignment, then the rest of us can go back to our own business. So practice all you like." He rolled over onto his side, yawned and curled up to take a nap. "No way are you going to make it past your apprentice test. When that happens, all this affirmative action fiddle-faddle will be nothing more than a memory."

Eloise sent him her most determined look, which, given her light-colored eyebrows and smooth features, probably wasn't all that fierce. But it was the best she could do.

No chubby-cheeked boy-toy wearing abbreviated wings and an oversize diaper was going to get the better of her or any other celestial female floating around. Women had rights, too, angels or not!

This guy certainly hadn't been much help teaching her to use a bow and arrow. All he'd done so far was sit on his fat…laurels!

She picked up her bow and sent an entire quiver of arrows right smack through the middle of the target one after the other.

"Hot damn!" Her hand flew to her mouth. *Oops!* Swearing was probably taking this liberation business a bit too far for an angel, particularly one of the lowest rank.

As she walked away from the archery range, she whistled a happy tune. At least she thought it was a happy tune. In harp school they'd told her instead of having "perfect pitch" she had "perfectly *awful* pitch." But she didn't mind.

She knew on *this* assignment she was going to be successful. A pioneer opening up new opportunities for celestial women everywhere. Besides, she loved visiting earth, and it had been some years since she'd had an opportunity. In this case, being a romantic at heart would definitely be a plus.

At long last she'd found where she belonged.

HUBERT LOOKED UP when Archie entered his office. "Did you have any luck?" he asked.

"No, sir. I tried my best to discourage her, but Eloise is amazingly determined. For a woman, that is."

"She's also the most inept angel in the entire universe. She can't possibly succeed."

"If she does, sir, everyone will realize exactly how easy our job is. If they do, they'll very likely downsize the entire department. We wouldn't want that, sir."

"No, we wouldn't." Thoughtfully, Hubert ran his palm across the top of his shiny head. "I'll simply have to take care of things myself, Archie. I won't let her out of my sight. She doesn't seem to realize that her two targets are totally unsuited for each other. It's impossible to imagine they would actually fall in love."

Archie gave his section chief a smug grin. "I should have had faith in you, sir. With you in charge, the department is in good hands."

Leaning back, Hubert placed his hands behind his head and gazed up at the ceiling dotted with mock stars. "I expect within the next millennium the authorities will recognize my administrative abilities and will promote me to a more important post. I'll need a good assistant then, Archie. What do you say?"

"I'd be honored, sir. Absolutely honored."

SPORT COAT SLUNG over his shoulder, suitcase in hand, Blake sprinted for the passenger ferry that served the string of small islands off the coast of

Georgia. He'd stopped by the hospital to check on Stevie, who was doing fine after his surgery. But Blake had cut his timing a little short. The ferry's departure whistle had already sounded.

He'd had to talk with the doctor about Stevie's prognosis. The doctor had said full recovery was only a question of time; the Billing Department made it clear it was a question of money.

More than ever, Blake was determined the promotion to vice president and the bonus that went with it would be his.

He leaped for the ferry just as a deckhand cast off the bowline. From the corner of his eye he had the impression of another body hurdling through space in the same direction. A body in a flowing white robe.

Distracted, he lost his footing as he grabbed for the railing. His suitcase came loose from his grip and skittered across the deck. His jacket slipped from his shoulder, floating downward to the widening sliver of dark water that separated the boat from the dock. At the same time the flying white form slammed into him and a feminine voice squealed in surprise.

"Oh, my gracious!"

Suddenly he was half sideways, the breath knocked out of him, dangling by one arm over the side of the ferry. And—arms and legs wrapped around his lower torso like a frightened centipede—there was a woman's face planted right smack-dab in his fly. With each ocean swell, his feet dipped closer to the water.

And his pants slipped down another inch.

2

"HEY, WHAT ARE y'all doing?" a crewman on board the ferry shouted.

"Lady?" Blake choked on the word as he looked down onto the top of a curly blond head. "Don't let go." Though the woman who had slammed into him didn't weigh much more than his nephew, her added weight was yanking his shoulder right out of its socket. Even worse, the placement of her face was having a predictable, if not yet visible, effect on a certain intimate part of his anatomy.

But he damn sure wasn't going to let her drop into the water. She'd probably take his pants with her.

Her flowing white sundress didn't offer much of anything to grab onto, so Blake hooked his free hand under her arm to stop her slow, sensual slide down his body. Her skin was as white as porcelain and so soft he wondered if the sun had ever kissed even an inch of her bare flesh.

Ever so cautiously, she lifted her head. Round blue eyes the color of cornflowers, framed by a halo of white-blond curls, snared him. Her lips formed a perfect *O*.

"Oops," she said. "Guess I almost missed the boat."

"Yeah, oops." With an effort he dragged his gaze away from the tempting sparkle in those blue eyes. Meeting a woman was definitely not part of his travel package for this trip. Strictly business, that's what he had on his mind.

Looking up at a pair of deckhands, who appeared to be stuck somewhere between laughter and paralysis, he asked, "Could we get some help here, guys?"

"Y'all sure do know how to make an entrance." Grinning, a big burly man with meaty hands knelt at the side of the boat and circled the woman's rib cage. "Come 'long, honey chil'. Y'all gotta let go or you both sure 'nough gonna be fish bait in a minute."

With an audible intake of air, the woman released her ferocious grip around Blake's hips and was lifted on board. Eased of her weight, Blake scrambled after her.

When he'd finally made it to his feet, he turned to the woman and said, "What the devil did you think you were doing? We could have both ended up in the drink."

"Heavenly days!" She looked shocked, as though her belated leap to the ferry hadn't been the least bit foolhardy. "I was trying to catch the boat just like you were. I couldn't get on board until I knew you'd make it, too."

"What does my making it have to do with—"

"Where y'all headed?" the beefy deckhand asked.

"Crankshank Island," they answered in unison.

Blake shot her a look. As far as he knew, the only people who'd be on the island this week were Crest's marketing managers, all of whom would be competing for the same promotion—the one *he* needed more than he needed to breathe. He frowned. She didn't look in the least familiar and he hadn't heard of any new directors being hired. "Which region are you from?"

She hesitated a moment, then said with a cute little grin, "Oh, the farthest region, I'm sure."

The Northwest, he imagined. Maybe even Alaska. Hell, it could be the Far East. Crankshank was always expanding his markets.

"Great. Glad you could make the trip." Good at playing office politics and eager for as many allies as he could enlist, he extended his hand. "Blake Donovan, southeast region."

"Yes, I know." Her hand had the same porcelain feel as her arm, fragile bones covered by warm velvet. Her cheeks were rosy without the need for so much as a smidgeon of makeup, reminding Blake of a china doll—or an angel. But if she was the marketing director of some new region, he didn't dare underestimate her.

"And you are?" he prompted.

"Eloise." She didn't release his hand. Perversely, he was pleased.

"Eloise…what?"

"Periwinkle. But everyone calls me Eloise. Except Hubert, of course. He likes to be more formal. Particularly with women, I think. We must make him nervous, though I can't imagine why. Women aren't all that difficult to deal with. Don't you agree?''

"Ah, sure." Uncharacteristically tongue-tied, Blake blinked. Who the hell was Hubert?

"Oh, dear. I hope I don't make you nervous."

That wasn't anywhere close to the reaction he was having. "Not a chance, sweetheart."

"I'm so glad because I've heard anxiety does terrible things to a man's libido. And I wouldn't want anything to damage yours for the next few days."

He eyed her speculatively. "I don't think that will be a problem."

The ferry had picked up speed, and the deck hummed beneath Blake's feet in sync with the diesel engines. His body was humming an interesting tune, too, one that had caught the rhythm of the wind tossing Eloise's curls around her face.

Sternly reminding himself he didn't mix business with pleasure, he released her hand. He needed to focus on the goal—the promotion and the bonus that went with it.

"Now that I've met you," she said, "I'm absolutely confident you believe a loving relationship between a man and woman is what we're all striving for."

"Did I say that?" He didn't think so; he didn't even believe it was possible, not based on the experience of his mother and his kid sister.

"I can see you're a romantic at heart. A man capable of both great compassion and great passion, with tons and tons of testosterone." She looked up at him with what appeared to be total innocence, which he didn't buy for a minute. "When you find that special woman—"

"Eloise, what the hell are you talking about? If you think you can bamboozle me into supporting you for the promotion—"

"What promotion?"

"To the Vice President of Marketing, of course. What else would I be talking about?"

"Heavens, I wouldn't want a job like that. I'm having enough trouble handling what they've already put on my plate."

"Yeah, I bet. You show up here, timing your arrival to coincide with mine, and now you're playing the sweet, innocent female with not a single wily scheme up her shirtsleeve. Well, I'm not buying it, sweetheart. You want that promotion as much as I do."

He followed her gaze as she looked down at her arms. They were nice arms, slender and graceful as she turned them from side to side. "I'm not wearing a shirt," she said, a puzzled frown tugging her pale blond brows together. "There's nothing up my sleeve."

Blake could see that. He didn't necessarily *want* to see that, but in a physical sense it was obvious. Meanwhile, his perfectly healthy libido agreed with his objective observation, to his growing discomfort. "Maybe we ought to go inside," he suggested, hoping she wouldn't. The ferry wasn't a large one but it did have an enclosed cabin for passengers, and several were milling about inside. At the moment, moving away from Eloise seemed like a particularly good idea.

She looked wistfully toward the islands that dotted the horizon only a few miles from the mainland. "Do we have to go inside? I love how everything smells here."

Smells? Blake hadn't given much thought to the tangy scent of sea salt that lingered at the back of his throat, or the way the air carried the distinctive aroma of grassy marshes that lay not far away. Those smells were simply a part of the short trip to the island. Hardly worth considering.

Except now he found them somehow more intriguing. There were layers of scent when he thought about it—the sea and marsh the most potent, but he detected the pungent odor of fish recently caught on the dock as well as a faint trace of azaleas and honeysuckle from the outer islands. Odd that he'd never noticed those distinctions before.

Not that he viewed them as having any great relevance.

But there was another scent, something vastly different from the natural environment of sea and marshlands. A faint yet heavenly scent so sweetly perfumed it made him ache with a longing for something he couldn't name. And didn't have time to identify.

He checked his watch. "Another ten minutes before we get to the island." And have to deal with Crankshank's latest scheme, he muttered silently.

"I'm going inside to make a call or two. You do whatever you want."

Discouraged, Eloise waited until Blake was out of sight before strolling to the front of the boat. She loved the feel of the wind in her face, the scents of sea and earth that were so different from her celestial atmosphere.

But she had not handled Blake Donovan at all well.

She'd been so excited about matching him with Margaret Wykowski, and so afraid he'd be a difficult case, she'd tried to sell romance too soon. She should have waited until she'd had the two of them together in the same room. Then her Cupid's arrows, carefully aimed and invisible to the human eye, would eliminate the need for any kind of a sales pitch. They'd be in love. She was confident the potion tipping her magic darts would be hard to resist. She wouldn't even need all of the allotted four days. One clean shot targeting each subject would do it.

The bow of the boat raised on a swell and a moment of regret trembled through Eloise.

She'd never before been so close to a human male. With her arms wrapped around him, she'd been intrigued by his ribbed belly and the rock hardness of his thighs. His arms were amazingly strong, too, holding her weight as easily as his own. She recalled that his eyes were the color of stormy clouds on the horizon and his hair as dark as midnight, his mouth sensual and inviting.

Inexplicably, his dark, brooding good looks had somehow set her off kilter.

She'd sensed a tension in him that was echoed somewhere low in her body. She had no idea what that meant, but it had caused a strange warmth to pass through her in spite of the chill air of the spring day. She really wished she could explore all of the fascinating ingredients that made up her new human form. And investigate the faint trace of loneliness she'd detected in Blake's dark eyes, in spite of his best efforts to cower her. But Hubert would unquestionably be displeased.

She had one job to do and one job only—to get Blake and Margaret to fall in love.

Blake was such a spectacular specimen of human maleness, she doubted Margaret would need much encouragement. Were it possible, Eloise imagined she could fall in love with him herself. Particularly since she knew so much about his admirable qualities.

But, of course, angels didn't have the capacity for romantic love. If they had, the whole universe would come to a screeching halt. Love, after all, had the power to send the world spinning out of control. Eloise wouldn't want that to happen, not on her account.

GULLS CRIED a noisy welcome, circling gracefully as the ferry approached Crankshank Island. The soaring cupolas of a gray, weathered house appeared above the curve of leeward sand dunes, a majestic sight as the setting sun caught the spires and reflected off tiny square panes of glass like priceless diamonds.

Blake was a lucky man, Eloise mused. Surely there could be no more romantic place in the world in which to fall in love. She sighed. Margaret was fortunate, too.

"You all set for the meeting?"

Eloise started at Blake's voice so close behind her. Smiling, she recovered quickly, placing her hand over the golden quiver and bow she had pinned to her dress. She fingered it gently, checking to see that all was in order.

"My sakes!" she cried, her eyes widening in horror. There were only two magic darts left in her quiver. The others must have fallen out and spilled into the water when she'd collided with Blake.

"What's wrong?" he asked.

"Nothing. I mean—" Dear goodness, what if she missed with her first shot? To be on the safe side, she really should have backup available.

"Hey, you'll be okay," Blake said, his gray eyes softening with sympathy. "Just don't let old Obadiah Crankshank intimidate you and you'll do fine. Trust me, his bark is worse than his bite."

"He barks?" How odd, she thought, distracted. *And bites, too?* But then, her only concern was hitting two fairly large targets. Staunchly she reminded herself how much her aim had improved of late. She was sure she'd be able to manage with only the remaining two darts.

"You know what I mean." Blake leaned against the railing, his back to the water, and folded his arms across his chest. The breeze caught his hair, fluttering the dark strands. Eloise noticed that his dramatic eyebrows were nicely arched, his nose straight and regal.

There was also a hint of a cleft marking an otherwise square chin.

"You know Mr. Crankshank well, I gather?" She didn't understand, of course, about people barking and biting. But confessing her ignorance seemed inappropriate at the moment.

"He gave me a chance when no one else would. I've never let him down. I won't if I get the promotion, either."

"Then for his sake, I hope you're the one who gets the job."

He tilted his head in a rather endearing way, like a little boy who knew he'd done something terribly wrong but wasn't going to have to take the blame. "Which region did you say you were from?"

The ferry bumped against the dock, jarring Eloise sideways. Right into Blake's arms. He looked down at her, a devilish spark of astonishment in his eyes.

Goodness, she hadn't realized a man's arms could feel so nice wrapped around her. Better than fleecy clouds, much warmer and far more secure. And he smelled of the tropics, a scent that was both tangy, rich and sweetly spiced.

He took her shoulders in his hands and set her more firmly on her feet. His mouth formed a stern line, but the corners of his lips quivered with the threat of a delicious smile. His eyes crinkled. "We've got to stop meeting like this, Ms. Periwinkle."

"I suppose you're right, Mr. Donovan."

"We are competitors, you know."

"I don't see it that way."

"Then how do you see it, Ms. Periwinkle?"

She swallowed hard, his unique human scent was teasing her senses. Her brain seemed to be taking a sabbatical, her thought processes turning to mush. "We could be friends," she suggested, though that wasn't exactly the subtext of the message his body was sending hers. Or what she saw in his stormy gray eyes. Or what she was feeling in every muscle, sinew and nerve ending of her own body.

"Friends?" He gave her a half smile, his gaze cruising intimately across her face before lingering boldly on her mouth. "In this business, everybody needs a friend."

Eloise thought she might never breathe again—wasn't sure she'd want to. *Oh, my, oh, my.* She mustn't fail on this assignment. The future of mankind and space exploration depended upon her, not to mention celestial affirmative action.

Chains rattled as the gangway clanked down onto the weathered dock.

"Crankshank!" a deckhand shouted. The other passengers remained in the cabin.

"We'd better go," Blake said, his eyes never leaving hers.

"Yes, of course," Eloise breathed, reminding herself that her job was to get Margaret and Blake together, to have them fall in love. An easy job, really. One that had been done thousands of times by apprentice cupids before Eloise. She could do this. She really could.

But she didn't necessarily have to like it.

Carrying his suitcase, Blake ushered her down the gangway to the dock, his hand warmly cupping her elbow. Her knees felt a little wobbly. No doubt her sea legs would take a moment to readjust to the land, she told herself.

But at the end of the dock, her feet came to a complete halt. She stumbled. Only Blake's firm grip on her elbow prevented her from falling.

Hubert? Her jaw went slack.

"Good evening, Miss." He bowed slightly, his shiny dome dipping toward her. "And Mr. Donovan, I believe?"

"That's right." Blake extended his hand. "You must be new."

"The regular butler has taken ill, sir. I'm from the agency. Hubert, sir. May I take your luggage, sir?"

Eloise sputtered. *A butler, my foot!* He's *spying* on me, for heaven's sake. "I could have done this on my own," she whispered for Hubert's ears only.

"I very much doubt that, my dear," Hubert replied in kind.

"Have you got a suitcase, Eloise?" Blake asked.

"Ms. Periwinkle's things arrived earlier, sir."

"They did?" she asked, surprised. What things? She wasn't planning to stay any longer than it would take to shoot the darts—once she got Blake and Margaret together.

"If you'll follow me, sir. Miss." Expressionless, Hubert turned and led them to an electric cart. His legs were so short, he had a decided wobble to his gait.

Eloise ground her teeth. Didn't Hubert think she could handle the job on her own? Or was he planning to sabotage her efforts? The whole future of celestial affirmative action depended on her success. No way was she going to let some gnome of a senior cupid mess up the future of women all across the universe.

Why, what would have happened if there hadn't been a female guardian angel watching over Madam Curie? She never would have discovered radium, that's what, and some man would have taken her rightful place in the history books.

There was also Blake's offspring to think about. He deserved his moment in the spotlight, too.

This time Eloise would get the job done. Hubert could take that and stuff it in his diaper.

BLAKE'S THIRD-FLOOR ROOM overlooked a landscaped yard featuring a towering flagpole—its flag snapping briskly in the sea breeze—and meandering paths that led down the bluff to the sea where a sheltered cove protected the mainland from storms. Crankshank's ancestral pirate had chosen his home base well. From this lofty perch he would have had a three-hundred-and-sixty degree view to protect him and his treasure from unexpected attack—assuming there was such a treasure.

Shrugging out of his dress shirt, Blake chose a jersey turtleneck from his suitcase and pulled it on. These marketing retreats were informal, focusing more on how to increase corporate sales—and succeed at Crankshank's bizarre games—than on how to dress for success.

More often than not, Crankshank's crazy games resulted in dismantling half the mansion or digging six-foot-deep trenches across the island. Blake had always suspected the destruction was part of his boss's scheme for cheap remodeling as well as his search for treasure.

In the adjacent room, Blake heard Eloise moving about. The connecting door, which lacked any sort of lock, remained firmly—though enticingly—closed. They had been the last two managers to arrive for the conference. The predinner cocktail party was about to commence.

He considered knocking on her door to invite her to go downstairs with him, but rejected the idea. It was smarter to go a little slowly with a new business associate, to wait to test the lay of the land and to see who was supporting whom for the promotion. A political misstep could cost him the job he coveted. And the bonus he needed.

He wished he could be at the hospital with Stevie now. The kid was courageous, but he was in a lot of pain. At least Blake knew Caroline was there. His primary job would be to make sure the boy got the best care possible, price no object. And that was damn well what he was going to do.

He checked his watch. Time to go.

Stepping into the hallway, he glanced at Eloise's door. She wasn't what he'd call a beautiful woman—too pixie-like with her upturned nose and cherubic cheeks. Other parts of her anatomy were nicely rounded, too—her breasts and the swell of her hips— but he didn't want to dwell on that. Business first was his motto. *Pleasure later,* he thought with a half grin before remembering that extracurricular activities weren't part of his agenda for the next few days.

As he made his way down the stairs, Blake noticed for the first time that the polished mahogany banister looked as if it had been made from the railing of an old ship and that the stairs were worn in the center as though thousands of feet had tread upon the steps. A gallery of portraits marched down the wall beside him to the lower floor; Crankshank sea captains, business moguls and their ladies.

He'd reached the bottom landing when a strange whooshing noise made him stop. He looked up the way he had come.

"Nooo..." he cried.

"Look out!" Eloise shouted. Her smile was the widest grin he'd ever seen as she plummeted toward him, sliding down the banister a thousand miles an hour, totally out of control. Her white skirt blew up around her thighs like a summer cloud, revealing shapely legs and slender ankles. White sandals flapped on her bare feet.

"You're going to get yourself—"

Flying off the end of the banister, she smashed right into him, driving the air from his lungs.

"Killed," he grunted, falling to the floor, Eloise landing on his chest.

"Wasn't that great! I've never done that before and

I've always wanted to.'' Her blue eyes sparkled like she'd kidnapped a skyful of fireworks. ''I tried once at the British Museum but the guard stopped me.''

He coughed and sucked in a ragged breath. He'd never met a woman quite so uninhibited, nor could he remember being quite so charmed. Her high spirits were absolutely infectious.

He forced himself not to smile. ''Have you ever considered showing a little restraint?''

''Not me. Life is too short.''

''Don't you think crashing into me three times in as many hours is a bit much?'' Though each time had been thoroughly enjoyable, if a bit unsettling. Damn, if this wasn't a business meeting…and Eloise a competitor for the job he wanted…

She wrinkled her upturned nose. ''I suppose you're right,'' she conceded, though without a great deal of remorse.

''Then maybe you'd at least think about getting off me.'' Before he did something foolish like take advantage of the situation and kiss her.

''Oh, sure.'' She twisted around, trying to get her feet under her, but her sandals slipped on the hardwood floor and sent her sprawling across him even more completely. Her hand ended up inches from his crotch, fingers squeezing his thigh, lighting a fire in him like a blowtorch.

At the same time all the ruckus they'd created by landing in a heap drew a crowd from the sitting room where the cocktail party was in full swing. The other managers had gathered in the doorway and stood peering down at Blake and Eloise. Their eyes were wide in a combination of curiosity and censure.

Hell of a way to start the retreat, Blake thought grimly.

Terry Turrell, hotshot marketing director from the upper Midwest region and an Ivy Leaguer, cocked one eyebrow. "I've always admired your technique with women," he said dryly.

"Yeah. Right." Blake clamped his hands around Eloise's waist and hefted her out of the way. At some distant level of awareness, he recognized that her waist was so slender he could almost span its circumference.

There was nothing graceful about the way he got to his feet, or how he helped Eloise to do the same.

"Hi, everyone," she said, giving their interested audience a dazzling smile as she smoothed her full skirt over her thighs. "I'm Eloise. It's nice to meet you."

Not one to let any grass grow under his feet, Terry stepped forward and offered his arm. "I have the feeling the pleasure is all ours, Eloise. Let me show you around. The hors d'oeuvres are especially delicious this year."

"Hors d'oeuvres?" she questioned.

"Snacks. You know, tasty morsels to nibble on." His tone, and the way he was ogling Eloise, suggested Terry was interested in nibbling on something other than food.

"Oh, good," she cooed, apparently oblivious to his innuendo. "I do hope they have some peanut-butter-

and-jelly sandwiches. That's my all-time favorite. You know, I once shared my sandwich with the cutest little kitty. She was so hungry but didn't seem to like peanut butter very much.''

Terry visibly did a double take. So did Blake. The woman was either totally nuts…or very clever at keeping competitors off balance. Blake's bet was on the latter.

The crowd of onlookers parted for them as Terry recovered his usual aplomb and ushered Eloise into the sitting room.

Blake followed them, nodding a greeting to familiar colleagues as he passed. He hated Terry's phony upper-class charm. The guy thought he owned the world simply because he'd been born with a silver spoon in his mouth. He had no idea what it meant to work to pay the rent and put bread on the table. Or what it was like to run a gauntlet of gang members just to get to school every day.

Blake had experienced all of that. He was stronger and more determined because of it. But it was at times like these, Blake thought, eyeing Terry and Eloise, he regretted that he no longer led with his fists.

In the sitting room Eloise felt the prickle of Blake's gaze along the back of her neck as Terry filled a plate with hors d'oeuvres for her.

"Do you like escargot?" he asked.

"Escargot?" she echoed. "Is that anything like peanut—"

"Snails. I think these are cooked in garlic and butter.''

"Oh," she said, disappointed. "I've always thought of snails as harmless creatures." Though nothing she'd particularly want to eat. Not that she'd thought of a feathery chicken as all that delectable either until she'd tasted one on her last trip to earth— her most recently botched guardian angel assignment.

Terry's laughter was a low rumble in his chest, making her wonder if Blake's laughter would be equally deep and rich.

Accepting Terry's gracious service, she selected a small square from the plate he'd filled and nibbled on something that tasted of artichokes and cheese. She sighed. Being able to eat real food was certainly a treat.

"Have you been to Georgia before?" Terry asked conversationally. She'd sneaked a peak at his files in the Record Department, just to make sure she'd know all the players when she arrived on earth. He was an interesting man. He'd always gotten exactly what he wanted, but had doubts that he deserved the easy life he led. She suspected he desperately wanted to prove himself.

"Is that where I am?" she answered, shrugging. "Borders don't mean much to me. I just travel wherever I'm sent."

"Then you must earn a lot of frequent-flyer miles."

She looked at him blankly. "I'm not sure anyone's actually keeping track of my mileage." Mercy, with only one trip the numbers would be in the gazillions.

And at the moment, she didn't have time for a lot of idle chitchat—or high math. She had work to do.

Glancing around the room, she spotted Hubert dressed in a white shirt and pants, with a sporty black bow tie added. Almost at the same instant her gaze landed on Margaret Wykowski. The only other woman in the room, she was strikingly tall, her blond hair pulled carefully into a sophisticated chignon, her makeup skillfully applied. In contrast, Eloise felt like the world's worst frump. No matter what she did, her wayward curls never behaved themselves.

It was obvious why Hubert and Cupid's Celestial Division had decided that Blake and Margaret would make the perfect couple. They both verged on physical perfection, though Eloise thought Blake had the advantage in that department. She found his stern features and expressive dark eyebrows slightly intimidating, and felt a delicious sense of danger whenever she looked at him...or found his arms wrapped around her.

Hubert gave Eloise an impatient gesture, as if to say, "Get on with it!" He started walking toward her.

"Oh, all right," she muttered. She picked up another morsel from her plate and popped it into her mouth, then licked a bit of butter from her fingers. She might as well enjoy as many interesting flavors as she could while she had the chance.

From the quiver pinned to her dress she plucked a single magic dart, one that only she—and presumably Hubert—could see. Blake stood only a few feet away talking with a distinguished gray-haired gentleman. At this range, he'd be an easy target.

She notched the arrow in her bow, drew back the

string, took a steadying breath and aimed. Then she let it fly.

Blake clamped his hand to the side of his neck right where she had aimed. *Bull's eye!* He looked around in search of what had hit him.

Now Eloise had to work quickly. The love connection could only happen with a woman who had also been stung by Cupid's secret potion. The elixir that was at this moment invading Blake's heart would wear off quickly if no matching bond was formed.

She notched her one remaining arrow, lifted the bow to aim and—

Someone bumped her arm. Hard.

Her fingers, already slick from the snack she'd eaten, slipped.

The arrow tumbled headlong from the bow, falling tip over golden feathers downward, spiraling to land point first.

"Ouch!" Eloise cried.

Good grief! She stared in dismay at the barb imbedded in *her* foot. The damn thing stung!

Her head snapped up, her hand covering her mouth, as her eyes met Blake's.

The connection was as powerful as an electric storm in the heavens, a lightning bolt sparked with magic. It sizzled through her right down to her toes. Her body shook with it; her heart nearly seized.

"Oh, *double* oops!" she groaned, the prospects of imminent failure looming large. She wasn't supposed to be the one compelled by Cupid's potion to fall in love.

From everything she was feeling, it didn't appear she was immune.

3

IN TWO STRIDES Blake crossed the distance to Eloise's side. She was hopping around on one foot, grimacing, as though someone had stepped on her toe.

"I love you," he murmured in her ear. The words were out before he could call them back. Stunned, he clamped his mouth shut. Why the hell had he said something so stupid? He didn't love Eloise. They'd only just met. In fact, he didn't want to love any woman. Ever. He'd resist that possibility with his last breath. No man needed that kind of grief. And he certainly had more important matters on his mind for the next few days.

He rubbed at the odd stinging sensation at the side of his neck.

"Are you two okay?" Terry asked, expertly balancing his glass of white wine on the edge of his plate. He was wearing a hand-tailored camel hair jacket and an expensive mock-turtleneck sweater that must have set him back megabucks.

"Yeah, fine," Blake muttered, unable to drag his gaze away from Eloise, still horrified by the ridiculous words he'd uttered.

Love, in his view, was nothing more than some

silly woman's fantasy—a dream that got a person into more trouble than anyone could handle, male or female. He'd have none of it.

Eloise's face had gone chalky white. Her eyes were huge as she looked up at him, all the while standing there like a one-legged stork. "It's a mistake. You didn't mean what you just said."

"You've got that straight, sweetheart." Except his heart was doing cartwheels, and he was more than a little breathless. He wanted to grab Eloise, toss her over his shoulder, and haul her upstairs to his room. Images of a warm, cozy house and smiling cherub-cheeked babies flashed into his mind. *His* babies— and hers.

He shook his head and rubbed at his neck. Somebody must have spiked his beer!

"I've heard the southeastern region has been going like gangbusters," Terry said. "I'm looking forward to hearing about—"

Ignoring Terry, Eloise hooked her hand through Blake's elbow and said, "Come on, I want you to meet Margaret. She's a beautiful woman. I know you'll love her."

Terry said, "I was just about to ask Eloise if she would care to sit with me—"

"Margaret and I have already met," Blake told her. The western regional whiz was right up near the top of Blake's list of things to avoid, along with black widow spiders and poisonous snakes. She'd crossed him not once but twice by landing big national accounts that should rightfully have been his.

"This time it'll be different," Eloise insisted, tugging him away from Terry and the hors d'oeuvre table.

Terry looked slightly bewildered, apparently unused to women not hanging on his every word.

"You'll be perfect together," Eloise told Blake. "You'll see."

Blake didn't think that was likely, but he did enjoy the feel of Eloise's hand on his arm, so he went along with her. It was too damn bad they were here on business...

"Hi, Margaret, I'm Eloise," she said brightly, almost breaking Blake's arm shoving him forward. "I love your dress. It's so...so sophisticated."

The slinky knit fabric clung to every one of Margaret's curves, and the deeply scooped neckline offered an enticing peek at cleavage probably enhanced with silicone.

"You're so lucky to be tall," Eloise continued. "You can disguise the extra weight you've put on. If I tried to wear something like that, every little bulge would show."

Margaret's glacial smile didn't reach her eyes. "Thank you for pointing that out."

"You look fine just as you are, Eloise," Blake said under his breath. *Like a ray of sunshine straight from the heavens,* he thought.

"Blake was telling me how much he admires you." Eloise nudged him with her elbow. "He wanted to come over and tell you himself but he's feeling a little shy right now."

With the yellow eyes of a cat, Margaret's assessing gaze raked him over, then her smile widened like the predator she was. "I didn't know you were bashful, Blake. You never let on."

"Yeah, well—"

"Dinner is served," Hubert announced from the doorway between the sitting room and dining area.

The buzz of conversation among the managers increased in volume as they sorted themselves out and entered the dining room in pairs or small groups.

The long table and sideboards were nineteenth-century period pieces, the dark polished wood glistening in the candlelight of the silver candelabra. Gold-velvet-flocked wallpaper and lush Oriental carpets muted the sounds. Overhead, heavy wooden beams spanned the breadth of the high-ceilinged room and two wrought-iron chandeliers dangled above opposite ends of the table.

Suddenly there was a lot of jockeying for position around Blake. He lost Eloise's hand on his arm. Someone shoved him forward down the row of waiting chairs.

When he came to a halt behind Spencer Doolittle of Colorado, he turned to find, not Eloise, but Margaret right behind him. He was trapped. He couldn't very well go pushing back the way he had come to find Eloise so that he could sit with her. Nor could he possibly squeeze past Spencer, who probably weighed three hundred pounds and filled every available space between the dining table and sideboard.

He smiled weakly at Margaret. "May I help you with your chair?"

"Of course, Blake. How very thoughtful of you. I didn't realize in addition to being a great manager, you're also a true gentleman."

"Yeah, well, I work at it." Right now he wished he hadn't bothered. Eloise had found herself a place across the table from him—and right next to Terry, who was also in the process of doing the gentlemanly thing by seating Eloise.

Blake didn't appreciate the twinge of jealousy that tweaked him somewhere near his spleen. That wasn't like him at all. He'd never had possessive feelings about any woman. This urge to leap over the table at Terry and punch his lights out was decidedly different. Totally inappropriate.

As they settled into their places—five people on each side of the table—Spencer suddenly asked of no one in particular, "So where's Mr. Crankshank?"

All heads swung toward the head of the table, the place the company president usually occupied.

The butler appeared from the kitchen, carrying a large soup tureen. "Mr. Crankshank won't be able to join you for a few days. He's asked that I make you all feel at home."

"You mean we're all gonna run this here executive meeting on our own?" David Ettienne from Mississippi asked.

"Maybe it means we won't have to play any of those fool games of Crankshank's and get some real work done instead," another manager suggested.

Hubert, the butler, smiled benignly as he ladled soup from the tureen. "There'll be a treasure hunt, as expected. But this evening you are to enjoy yourselves. Tomorrow will be soon enough to begin your search. It should prove quite amusing, I assure you."

There was general groaning among the troops, but Blake knew most of his fellow workers enjoyed the challenge of Crankshank's games. It honed their competitive edge. Success often turned out to be both lucrative and good for their careers. They'd all play the game.

Blake was determined to play it better than anyone else. Stevie was depending upon him. One of the last things the boy had said to him before Blake had left for the retreat was how much he wanted to be a pro baseball player some day. That meant his ankle would have to heal perfectly. Blake would do his part to give the kid the chance.

But concentrating on his goal was damn hard. His gaze kept drifting across the table to Eloise. Margaret said something to him but he was so distracted he had to ask her to repeat her question.

"I asked if you'd had a chance to line up Snappy Pizza yet."

He frowned. "Why would you ask that?"

"Because we're both addicted to the *Wall Street Journal* and Snappy is expanding here in Georgia."

"*My* territory," he reminded her. "My man in Savannah signed 'em on the dotted line this afternoon." Apparently just in time, or Margaret would have gone after the account. She was not averse to stretching territorial limits.

"How nice for you." She smiled none too sweetly.

From across the table, Eloise asked, "What sorts of things do you like to do when you're not at work, Margaret?"

"Well, I…" She hesitated. "My parents and I have season tickets to the opera. Do you by any chance enjoy—"

"No, I'm more an instrumentalist by training. The harp, actually. But Blake loves opera, don't you?"

He opened his mouth in surprise. "Me? I've never even been to an opera. It'd probably put me right to sleep."

Margaret sniffed her disapproval.

Eloise looked equally disappointed but quickly recovered. "When you're not going to the opera, then what do you do?" she prodded.

"I'm on the board of the arboretum. It's a worthy cause and certainly a good place to make contacts."

"I like trees and flowers," Blake offered, eager not to disappoint Eloise again.

"There, you see!" She beamed at him. "I knew you and Margaret would have a lot in common. Now you tell her what you enjoy doing in your spare time, Blake."

He frowned at Eloise, then turned and frowned at Margaret. She frowned back at him. "I've got a nephew in Little League. I coach when I have a chance."

Margaret turned her attention to the bowl of soup Hubert had delivered. "I find baseball deadly dull."

Eloise's expression crumbled.

"I was a pretty good third baseman in high school," Blake said, more eager to impress Eloise than Margaret. "Batted better than three-twenty-five my junior year." That was before he had to drop out of school and go to work to feed his family.

"You *hit* three hundred and twenty-five people?" Eloise gasped in surprise.

"No," he said patiently, though he wanted to laugh. "That means when I came to bat I *got* a hit almost a third of the time."

"They hit *you?*" she asked with even more dismay.

He shook his head. Eloise was either not much of a sports fan, or she came from some other planet. "How 'bout if I explain later?"

"Well, I'm sure whatever you did, you were wonderful." She sighed and smiled.

Blake felt that smile clear down to his pants.

A master at the game of one-upmanship, Terry said, "I played club soccer at Dartmouth. We were undefeated my senior year." He leaned forward, his soup spoon like a baton in his hand. "Speaking of opera, I was in Vienna a few days last year during the season. It was glorious. Marvelous costuming and superb voices."

That caught Margaret's attention but, to Blake's relief, it didn't seem to stir Eloise's interest. He had no idea what she was up to. Or why she'd care a fig about Margaret's interests.

What he wanted was for Eloise to be interested in him—which was ridiculous. He didn't have time for a relationship with a woman. And she didn't look like the type willing to settle for a one-night stand. If it weren't for his concern for his nephew, *he'd* certainly be willing to consider it.

There was a sweet innocence about her that was strangely refreshing. While Margaret was sophisticated and cool, Eloise was open and honest. He could see it in her guileless eyes. Her quick smile lit up a room like a lighthouse on a dark night.

Most of the men in the room had already noticed, even those who were happily married. They kept eyeing Eloise just the way Blake did—with curiosity, fascination...and hunger.

In fact, as dinner progressed, he grew less and less interested in the meal, and more and more inquisitive about the flavor of Eloise's bowed lips. He wondered when he'd have a chance to taste them. In spite of knowing that was a bad idea, he promised himself it would be soon.

AFTER THE MEAL Eloise slipped away from the others, pursuing Hubert into the kitchen. Two women, one quite rotund and the other petite, were handling the cleanup chores. The heavyset woman had her arms buried in soapsuds clear up to her elbows.

Eloise gave her an encouraging smile, then whirled into the pantry, close on Hubert's heels. She refused to believe what she was feeling for Blake was love. Immune or not to the magic potion, she wasn't going to let her emotions ruin her chance for success on this assignment.

"I'm going to need more darts," she confessed to Hubert. Dinner had not gone well. Clearly, Margaret had no interest in Blake—and his feelings also seemed to lack romantic spark. All she had managed was to maneuver the seating arrangement so they were next to each other. Hardly an auspicious beginning.

Stretching, Hubert placed a tin of strawberry herbal tea on a high shelf barely within his reach. "You had ample resources at your disposal when your assignment started. Waste is not considered a worthy attribute where we come from."

"Yes, I know that. But when I jumped onto the ferry, most of them fell out. And then I missed—"

"Did you now?" he asked dryly. He eyed her with considerable disdain. "Why am I not surprised?"

"I was right on target with Blake and then something happened. I…" Her forehead scrolled into a frown, her words slowing as she recalled what had happened. "Someone bumped my arm. Hard. I dropped…" But maybe that bump hadn't been entirely accidental. Hubert had never wanted her to succeed as an apprentice cupid. He'd been dead set against her getting the job.

She planted her fist on her hip. "Now listen, buster. I want to know the truth. Were you the one who made me miss my aim so you could say 'I told you so'? If you were, I'm going to report you to—''

''I was nowhere near you, Ms. Periwinkle.''

She wasn't so sure that was true but she couldn't very well call a senior cupid a liar. Besides, her memory of the event was a bit hazy. She'd been too disoriented by the rush of feelings that had sped through her the moment the dart had penetrated her foot. Mercy, they ought to issue steel-tipped shoes to cupids when they're sent on assignment. ''Well, it could have been some magical thing you did,'' she concluded lamely.

''Has it ever occurred to you that your failure is due entirely to your own incompetence? In all the millennium you've been a celestial being, you have shown not one whit of aptitude for any of your assignments. Your continued failure comes as no surprise at all.''

The blood drained from Eloise's face. ''I haven't failed this time. Not yet. The potion is still working on Blake.'' He'd looked at Eloise with such love in his eyes, her faith in his capacity for grand passion had been more than validated. Of course, she was the *wrong* woman... ''And I'm sure if I just had one more—''

''There are no additional resources available. You must solve the problem with whatever you already have.''

''But I don't have—'' The only resource Eloise had was herself, which wasn't saying a great deal, she admitted. But she did have determination—that ought to count for something—and she had pluck. Everyone she'd met had commented on that. She'd always tried hard, too. For instance, the fact that she was a little tone deaf shouldn't have mattered so much in the harp orchestra. Even the conductor had conceded she'd given it her all.

Smirking, Hubert brushed past her, returning to the kitchen. "I'm confident, in due time, we will be able to find a *qualified* cupid to compensate for your failure."

"Now wait a minute." She stormed out after him. "I haven't given up yet. Just because you've been planning all along that I would mess up this job just like I've done all the others, doesn't mean it's over yet." She could have pinched herself for admitting she'd messed up in the past, particularly when Hubert arched his brows. Besides, even though she'd been forced to stretch a rule or two in the past didn't mean she'd totally failed. "I'm going to keep trying."

His chubby shoulders lifted in an indifferent shrug. "As you wish, Ms. Periwinkle. My staff will be there to pick up the pieces when you finally resign yourself to the inevitable."

Phooey! she thought, fuming. Nothing was inevitable. To succeed, a person just had to keep on trying.

"Now, if you will excuse me…" Hubert straightened his spiffy black bow tie. "I must inform the guests of the rules of tomorrow's game. I suggest you run along. Your attendance is not required."

Determined not to let Hubert dismiss her so easily, Eloise tagged along after him.

In the sitting room she discovered clutches of people standing in groups of two or three. Blake and Margaret were at opposite sides of the room, totally ignoring each other.

Heavens, but she had her work cut out for her. And she didn't dare let her own emotions get in her way, in spite of the quick lurch of her heart when she caught sight of Blake.

BLAKE KNEW the moment Eloise came into the room. Though he'd been talking with Spencer for several minutes, he felt Eloise's presence like a warm caress down his spine or like the soft brush of lips across his mouth. The faint trace of her sweet, heavenly scent teased his senses.

In stunned awareness, he realized he'd been waiting for her, wondering where she was and wanting to be there, too. Wherever she was.

But he needed to stay away from her.

At some intuitive level, he knew she was dangerous, and so were the feelings she engendered in him. Not just the lust part. He could probably handle that. Even enjoy acting on the sharpening of desire he'd been experiencing since before dinner.

But he also suspected she could make him forget his priorities. That would be disastrous, particularly during this critical time in his career. And in Steve's life.

Even as he warned himself of all the pitfalls that lay in Eloise's direction, his feet moved of their own accord toward her, not away.

Spencer stopped him. "So maybe we can work together on the treasure hunt this year?" He popped a chocolate candy into his mouth, his fifth in as many minutes. "We'd make a good team."

"Let me think about it, okay?" Usually Blake worked alone. He preferred it that way. The glory— or failure—in whatever task he set himself would be his own.

"Gentlemen. Ladies." Hubert had planted himself in the middle of the room, directly between Blake and Eloise. In his hands were several small, white envelopes. "These are the initial clues with which you will begin the treasure hunt tomorrow morning. Each clue is different. You will each be searching for a different series of clues so that your paths should not at any time cross until you reach the final step in the game."

So far the rules sounded the same to Blake as in prior years; Crankshank's odd exercise in team building and employee bonding, which often resulted in near destruction of the Crankshank mansion. He tried to peer around Hubert to catch a glimpse of Eloise, wondering what her reaction was to this business. But all he could see of her was one bare arm and a sandaled foot. He felt like he was viewing a peep show, and he wanted to see more.

"Should you conclude you are not able to locate any clue within the allotted time period—which is noted on the clue card—you will find there is a smaller, sealed envelope inside. You may open it to continue the game, but at your peril."

"That's when the pirate leaps out at us with his

sword in hand and makes us walk the plank, right?''
Terry suggested.

There was general tittering among the managers.

Hubert didn't so much as crack a smile. Neither
did Blake.

"You are permitted to form teams, if you so desire," the butler continued. "Or, of course, you may
work alone."

"I pick Eloise," Terry announced, his grin one step
short of being salacious.

"I don't blame you," the guy from Washington
State said. "I'd flip you for the chance, but I think
my wife might object."

The tension-easing laughter was a little louder this
time.

A muscle in Blake's jaw began to twitch.

Hubert waited until the room quieted. "Each team
member, however, must reach the final step of the
game simultaneously in order to qualify for the grand
prize."

"Not very likely more than one person's going to
get promoted," Ettienne muttered.

"I'm afraid Mr. Crankshank has not revealed the
details of his plans to me."

Crankshank's clues also tended to be ambiguous,
Blake recalled. The game's details were enough to
drive a man—or woman—crazy. Little wonder the
situation sometimes got out of hand.

Others started asking Hubert questions about the
treasure hunt but he gave them no help beyond what
he had already told them.

Behind the butler, a bit more of Eloise's shoulder and some of her white-blond curls appeared. Blake edged to the right, pushing Spencer out of the way so he could get a better view.

After several minutes of unproductive discussion, Hubert handed out the envelopes.

Blake took his and ripped it open. Before he checked inside, he looked around. Everyone appeared to be holding their cards close to their chests.

Ettienne groaned when he read his.

"Here we go again," Spencer moaned.

Glancing to his closest neighbors to be sure no one was sneaking a peek over his shoulder, Blake slipped his card from its envelope. The printed words he found were cryptic—*Rise with the sun*—with a notation that the next clue must be found before the noon meal.

As a marching order for tomorrow, that was fine with Blake. Knowing Eloise was in the room adjacent to his, with only an unlocked door between them, he doubted he'd get much sleep anyway.

But he didn't have the vaguest idea what the words meant in terms of where his next clue was hidden. He only knew he needed the answer before lunch tomorrow or he'd earn a handful of penalty points.

He didn't intend to let that happen. Not this year.

4

AFTER THE MEETING had broken up and everyone had gone to their rooms, Eloise pushed open the connecting door from her room to Blake's. "I have this really good idea how you can—"

Her feet came to a halt midstride, and her eyes widened. Blake had taken off his shirt and was standing next to the bed, his belt unbuckled, his fly unzipped. Fascinating swirls of dark hair covered his chest, tapering toward his narrow waist. She hadn't realized—

"Maybe next time you should knock first." He zipped up his pants and grabbed his shirt from the foot of the bed.

"Oh, sure." But then she would have missed the intriguing sight of Blake half naked, she thought as he hastily pulled the soft, clingy shirt over his head. In her mind's eye, she could still see the light furring of hair she'd spotted, and her fingers itched to discover what it felt like. She blinked the image and the errant thought away. "It's just that I didn't get a chance to talk to you downstairs, and I thought before you went to bed we ought to make some plans for tomorrow."

"Plans?"

"About how you're going to find the treasure."

His eyebrows pulled together. "I usually work alone, Eloise."

"Well, see, I don't think you should this year." She crossed the room and sat on the side of the bed. It was a big four-poster made of dark wood with a silk canopy above it, much like the one in her own room but in richer, more masculine colors. The soft mattress gave beneath her weight. "So what was the first clue Hubert gave you?"

He looked at her suspiciously. "Something about rising with the sun."

"Do you know what it means?"

"Not even close. It's supposed to be hard to figure out."

She nodded, causing her curls to rub against her cheek. "I knew it. What you need is a really smart partner so you can figure out all these clues and be the first to find the treasure."

"I see." Blake leaned against a bedpost, intrigued by the way she made herself at home in his room. After the butler had distributed the first round of clues, Eloise had been surrounded by half the managers vying for her as their partner. Blake hadn't been able to get anywhere near her so he had decided to call it a night and save his energy for the treasure hunt instead. Now here she was sitting on his bed, and the search for clues was damn far from his mind. He could think of a lot of other activities he and Eloise could enjoy together, none of which requiring that they leave the room. But he shouldn't be thinking about that.

"I gather you think you'd be the perfect partner for me." In bed or out? he wondered.

"Oh, not me." She smiled up at him with lips so full and ripe they looked as though they'd been made for kissing. "I wouldn't be any good at all on a treasure hunt."

"You wouldn't?" The other ideas he had in mind might be right up her alley, however.

"Well, I don't actually know that because I've never tried. But I was once assigned to find a man who was lost in the deepest, darkest part of Africa. I looked for ages and ages, but someone else found Dr. Livingstone before I did." She twisted her lips into a self-deprecating smile. "I got more lost than he was. A lot of the projects I try aren't totally successful."

Cute, really cute. This babe was a real jokester. "Guess this week will be just another grand adventure for you then."

"It already has been. And I'll certainly help you figure out the clues, if I can. But Margaret's the one you ought to have as a partner. She's about as smart as they come, knowing all that stuff about opera and trees and things. I think you ought to snap her up as a partner before somebody else asks her."

He looked at her blankly. "What's with you and Margaret? Has she put you up to this?" If so, Blake would bet a big chunk of his bank account that Margaret had a scheme cooking. "Don't let yourself be a patsy for her. You have to think of your own career, too.''

"That's exactly what I'm doing," she said with a cute little twist of her lips. Placing her hands behind her and locking her elbows, she leaned back on the bed. The action stretched the bodice of her white dress across her chest, drawing attention to her gently rounded breasts and the gold pin she perpetually wore, a miniature bow and quiver. Her feet didn't quite reach the floor, and she kicked them as if she were filled with a restless energy she couldn't quite contain.

Blake had trouble concentrating on the conversation. He really should be calling Caroline to see how Stevie was getting along. He would, too, as soon as he figured out what Eloise was up to.

"Then why don't you try to find the treasure for yourself?" he asked. "Crankshank would be impressed if a first-timer beat out the rest of us. He might even give you the promotion."

"Oh, I'm not eligible."

"You're not?" Crankshank had been known to make even screwier decisions than to promote Eloise. In fact, having her for a boss didn't seem all that bad a choice. She already had half of Crest's executives wrapped around her little finger—Blake included. Though getting any work done with her around might be a problem for any one of them—except Margaret, of course. Eloise was so damn sexy and innocent all at once, it would be hard for a man to keep his thoughts focused on the job.

"No, I'm, uh, too new with the company to be considered for promotion," she said. She stood, bringing the top of her head to his chin, and her sweet, heavenly scent to his nose. "But either Margaret or you would be perfect. That's why the two of you should show a united front. You know, the two top managers working shoulder to shoulder for the good of the company. That sort of thing."

"A nice image, but Margaret has her own agenda. I doubt she'd be interested in working with me."

"Could you be judging her too harshly? Maybe it's harder for a woman to succeed in a man's world, and what you're seeing is simply her determination. I know sometimes I feel that way."

"Maybe," he conceded. He understood about ambition—and moving up the corporate ranks had to be tough for a woman—so maybe he ought to cut Margaret a little slack. But she'd also burned him more than once by moving into his territory.

"There, I knew you really liked Margaret. And I'm sure she'll be tickled to work with you if you ask her." Eloise seemed quite pleased thinking he'd moderated his opinion of Margaret.

Blake hated to disappoint her. "Based on what I know of Margaret, she's probably out there now—" he gestured toward the darkness beyond the open window, a cool breeze fluttering the lacy curtains "—trying to get a head start on the rest of us."

"But Hubert said no one was to start the game until morning. She wouldn't break the rules, would she?"

Blake raised his brows. How the devil had anyone

as naive as Eloise survived for so long? "Let's take a look." He slipped his arm around her—mostly because he had a nearly irresistible desire to touch her—and ushered her to the window. She fit beside him as if she'd been perfectly designed to snuggle against him on cold winter nights.

The rising moon cast ribbons of silver across the open water, which undulated with each ocean swell and finally tumbled in a wave-driven froth onto the beach. Eloise's hair curled in a matching shade of silver-blond, but appeared softer and far more inviting to the touch.

His heart beating hard, Blake dipped his head toward those inviting curls, wanting to—

"Oh, my sakes!" Eloise gasped. "There she is!"

Following Eloise's gaze, Blake caught sight of a furtive figure dashing across the open ground toward a cluster of wind-sculpted cypress, and then it vanished into the shadows.

"Like I told you," Blake said, returning his attention to the far more interesting sight of Eloise's pulse beating wildly at her temple. Perhaps she wasn't immune to him after all. "Margaret doesn't let any grass grow under her feet when there's a career move at stake." His voice was rough with wanting.

Eloise turned in his arms, her face only inches from his, her lips—

"She's cheating." Her words were a shocked whisper.

His gaze locked on hers, he shrugged. "Looks like it."

"But her chances for promotion would be ruined if she got caught."

"Very possibly." It wasn't an issue that concerned him at the moment. It should have, damn it! But it didn't. Not with Eloise standing so close.

"Then you have to stop her." Lifting her chin, Eloise's determined expression was so fierce, Blake could only wish her interest in him was equally as strong. "Margaret will thank you for it. I'm sure she will."

Blake wasn't nearly so confident. "Look, Eloise, in some ways I admire what Margaret has accomplished. Her region has a dynamite record, and as far as I know, her people are immensely loyal to her. And her clients are certainly satisfied. But that doesn't mean I have to be her keeper."

"Yes, it does," Eloise muttered under her breath. She had to find some way to get Blake and Margaret together—at least as close as *she* and Blake were standing now—his arms looped gently around her, his chest mere inches from hers. Then nature would surely take its course in the same way she wanted to sink her fingers into his shirt, reach up on tiptoe to place a kiss on his lips, feel his long, lean body pressed up against the length of hers. What woman could possibly resist?

"Come on," she said, ducking away and slipping her hand in his.

She hurried him out of the room and down the flight of stairs. Moments later they were outside running across the well-manicured lawn past the flagpole toward the stand of cypress.

"Isn't it a lovely evening?" she said, breathless as she smiled up at him.

"It's a little chilly, don't you think?"

"Oh, no, I'd much rather have it too cool than too hot." Hot places were definitely frowned upon where she came from. But she liked the warm feel of Blake's hand in hers. Warm and pleasant. And she hated to let go. It must surely be the aftereffect of Cupid's potioned dart that had her heart beating a more jazzy rhythm than had ever been allowed in harp choir.

"Hey, where are you two going?"

Blake brought Eloise up short at the sound of a man's voice. "I could ask the same of you, Terry. What are you doing out here?"

Hands in his pockets, Terry ambled toward them. "I couldn't sleep. Must be the time change. Or more likely, I'm feeling a little nervous about tomorrow," he admitted.

Given Terry's need to prove himself, Eloise suspected that might be true. Poor man. But right now she was more concerned about Margaret. By now she could be halfway to the far end of the island.

Blake clung firmly to Eloise's hand. "I don't suppose you could be trying to get a leg up on the rest of us by tracking down your first clue a little ahead of the starting whistle?"

"Not me," Terry said, all innocence. "But I might have spotted you from the porch and come to warn Eloise not to put all her eggs in your basket."

"*Eggs?*" she asked, glancing around. *What* eggs? What *basket,* for that matter?

"Blake doesn't have a chance of coming out the winner in ol' Crankshank's game," Terry said, slipping back into his mask of confidence. "He's never even come close in all the years I've known him."

"That's not true," Blake objected, scowling.

"Now *me,*" Terry continued, "I've got a winning track record. Anyone in marketing who hooks up with me is going to be riding high, mark my words. Particularly a pretty little lady like you."

"Buzz off, Turrell. Eloise is with me."

"No, I'm not. Well, I am, but—"

"Smart move, Eloise, dumping a loser," Terry said.

"Blake isn't a loser." Eloise bristled at Terry's put-down. The game hadn't even started and he was already declaring himself the victor. It was like Hubert being convinced she wouldn't succeed before she'd even had a chance to try. "You'll see. Why, he's so smart he'll find the treasure in no time."

Terry looked skeptical.

So did Blake. "It's getting late, Eloise. Let's call it a night."

She didn't want to, since she hadn't made an iota of progress toward getting Margaret and Blake together. But she didn't want to stand there discussing with Terry how wonderful Blake was and how her heart did a little somersault every time she looked at him.

Sighing, she said, "Good night, Terry. If you see

Margaret, tell her..." *That she's missing her big chance to fall in love with a pretty terrific man.*

"See you in the morning, Eloise," Terry said, a gleam in his eyes. "Dream of me."

She doubted Terry would be the one who to inhabit her dreams tonight.

She and Blake went back into the house, walking up the wide staircase side by side, her hand still in his, warm and comforting and extraordinarily masculine. In the hallway, he stopped in front of the door to her room.

"Maybe you ought to listen to Terry."

She looked at him in surprise. His gray eyes had darkened to midnight black, the intensity in them so powerful it took her breath away. "Why would I want to do that?" she whispered.

"Because he's right that I've never won one of these treasure hunts. I came close last year, but close doesn't necessarily count in this business. You might be better off—"

"No, you're wrong. This year is going to be different. I know it is."

His lips slid into a wry grin. "I don't think anybody has stuck up for me like you did with Terry since my kid sister jumped on the back of some schoolyard bully who was beating me to a pulp. It surprised him so much, he let me up. Fortunately I was able to return the favor a few years later when some other bozo was giving Caroline a hard time."

A band of pure emotion tightened around Eloise's heart. "Good for you. *And* your sister."

"Yeah. She's a pretty terrific lady. So's her kid." He lifted his hand, his fingertips caressing Eloise's cheek, his voice low and raspy. "And so are you."

A heavenly warmth seeped through her body. *Temptation,* she recognized with a delicious start. No wonder mere mortals succumbed so easily.

She licked her lips. "I think we'd better say goodnight." She'd been warned about the dangers angels faced when mixing with mankind. But she'd never before experienced such a surge of desire to reach for the forbidden fruit. Perhaps later—much later—she'd discuss the problem with Hubert.

At the moment it seemed much more important to simply escape into her room and secretly savor these new and exciting feelings, hug them to herself before she made any incriminating confessions.

Hubert did not appear to be a particularly understanding boss.

"MORNING GLORIES."

"What?" Blake's head swiveled around to look at Eloise. They were standing on the porch that extended the width of Crankshank's mansion. Or rather, Blake was standing on the porch. Eloise was walking barefoot along the porch railing, ducking past the old cast-iron bell that called the guests to meals, her arms outstretched as she balanced herself, the picture of a woman enjoying a few moments of uninhibited fun. Blake envied her ability to enjoy everything she did. She lived in the moment, apparently without care for the future.

At first light she'd come with him to the kitchen, interrupting the cooks at work, burying her hands in the rising bread dough like a child playing with clay for the first time. She hadn't found the clue Blake had thought might be there, but she'd laughed and smiled, and somehow he hadn't minded that the first place they'd looked hadn't been the right one.

Then he'd found a newspaper that had been delivered by the dawn ferry. She'd peered over his shoulder as he searched the columns for the clue he was after, her breath sweet on his cheek. She'd sighed sadly at a story of a terrorist bomb killing innocent children in a far-off land and laughed at the photo of a wirehaired terrier wreathed in spring flowers.

He'd been tempted to linger, simply enjoying her company. By force of will, he'd dragged himself back into the game.

Now the urge to linger was back, even more powerfully. He *had* to fight it. Winning meant everything!

Like a dancer listening to music only she could hear, Eloise spun around the post at the end of the porch and dropped to the weathered deck. "Morning glories rise with the sun."

"You're right. But have you seen any morning glories around here?"

"No, but there ought to be some. I mean, this whole island is a garden. There're so many flowers blooming, the air is filled with their scent."

The only scent that interested Blake was hers. He couldn't seem to get enough of it and found himself trying to stay close to her so he would catch a sweet, heavenly whiff. "In the absence of any other idea, let's give it a try," he told her.

Like an eager child off on a school holiday, she asked, "Which way shall we go?"

"I saw Spencer heading toward the lagoon, and Terry is rummaging around in the basement. Ettienne and Margaret looked like they were going toward the southern tip of the island."

"Oh, good. Let's go that way." Grabbing his hand, she tugged him off the porch.

When they reached the path and Eloise headed south, Blake hauled her back. "Margaret has probably convinced Ettienne to go in with her on the search. We'll go north."

"But Margaret is—"

"Precisely. Hubert said the clues are arranged so our various paths shouldn't cross. That means we need to go in the opposite direction."

Her shoulders slumped. "I suppose you're right." She was really sorry to hear Ettienne and Margaret might be working together. If they developed a romantic relationship—and Margaret was certainly a gorgeous woman—Eloise's mission would be totally botched. And poor Blake would have no one. Eloise desperately didn't want that to happen. He deserved a woman to love. After all, his file made it clear that he was a hard worker, devoted to his job. And he loved his sister and nephew. That ought to count for a whole lot. But he wouldn't earn his just reward if she couldn't somehow find a way to get him together with the woman who was intended to be his lifetime partner.

And then there was his unborn son to worry about. If Eloise couldn't get Margaret and Blake together, the entire future of space exploration would be stunted.

A shiver went through Eloise and an odd press of tears burned the backs of her eyes. There was no reason at all she should regret that the woman who bore Blake's child wouldn't be her.

BEYOND THE LANDSCAPED gardens, grass grew in clumps, holding the dunes together. The wind blew constantly across the island, though gently now in the soft morning air. It teased Eloise's hair around her face, molded her skirt against her thighs.

Rubbing his hand along the side of his neck, Blake decided he was going crazy. He'd never wanted to be with a woman as much as he wanted to be with Eloise. It was as though a drug had invaded his system, a drug he didn't want to resist. But he would. Mixing business and pleasure were a lethal combination.

Like a nymph returning to the sea, Eloise ran down the sandy dune to the waves lapping on the beach.

"Take off your shoes," she cried, wading ankle-deep into the water, her sandals dangling from her fingers. "It feels wonderful."

"We're supposed to be looking for that damn clue." She was the most free-spirited corporate executive he'd ever met and sorely tempted a man to break his vow to find his pleasure a long way from the office. Of course, this was half a state from his offices in Atlanta...

"Oh, I know. But just for a minute." She kicked at the water, spraying it toward him and up on her skirt in big, wet circles.

What could it hurt if he indulged himself—and Eloise—a little? He hadn't gone barefoot since he'd been a kid. He'd never had the time.

He took off his shoes and socks and curled his toes into the damp, gritty sand. She smiled at him, the sparkle in her blue eyes pure devilment.

"You like this?" he asked.

"There aren't any beaches where I come from."

"I haven't been to the beach in more years than I can remember."

"If I lived here, I think I'd come all the time." She pirouetted in place, then bent and in one graceful motion scooped up a handful of water and tossed it right smack in his face.

"Why, you—"

"Oops!" Giggling, and clearly not at all remorseful for splashing him, she ran off down the beach— a playful minx, a little devil, an irresistible angel.

"I'll get you for that," he warned. His laughter was rough and rusty from disuse, his strides lacked her lithe grace as he pursued her. Her light footsteps barely left a print in the sand; his sank far deeper, slowing him. But he wasn't about to let her get away.

He caught her where the beach narrowed and turned west at the northern tip of the island. She stumbled, but he was there to catch her, rolling under her to break her fall. She was laughing hard, her eyes bright, her cheeks glowing rosy in the morning air.

"Oh, my," she sighed, breathing fast.

He sighed, too, feeling the weight of her body along the length of his, the press of her breasts against his chest as she breathed in and out. He slid his fingers into her curls, kneaded her scalp. Time seemed to stand still, shimmering on waves of intangible anticipation. Her lips were so close, her scent so captivating. Erotic. "You're beautiful."

Her eyes widened. "No, that's not true." Her musical voice was hardly more than a whisper, a soft clarion that could carry across a perfectly designed church—or reach into a man's heart.

"But it is true. I should know. I'm the one looking at you."

"No one else has ever thought so."

"They're blind, then." And he had eyes only for her; he was obsessed with her. Drugged by her.

A shadow of what Blake thought might be sorrow filled her eyes before she slipped from his grasp and jumped to her feet as if she'd recalled some desperate mission she had to accomplish.

"Look, we've found them! Morning glories." She scrambled up the embankment where wild vines loaded with white and blue blossoms entwined through the breeze-blown oat grass. Touching one blossom lightly, lifting the bloom with only her fingertips, she smiled—almost sadly—and said, "They're like angel's trumpets."

Disoriented, Blake followed her up the slope.

There'd been magic in the air and now there was an emptiness he didn't understand.

He checked his watch. Damn it! Why was he having so much trouble concentrating? "We'll have to hurry. If we don't find the next clue before lunch is served I'll end up with penalty points."

Looking around at the acre of vines and blossoms and blowing grass, she shook her head. "I don't know…"

"Let's give it a shot." There wasn't much else Blake could think of to do, so they started searching through the morning glories like children on an Easter egg hunt.

"Have you ever been in love?" Eloise asked from a few feet away.

His hand froze on a piece of driftwood. "I've never had time for stuff like that."

"How long could it take?"

Longer than he'd ever had—until now. "If you're looking for wine and roses, you're looking in the wrong place, Eloise. I don't believe in any of that. My mother and sister did. They were played for fools. Love is nothing more than a fantasy."

Eloise brought a morning glory to her face, rubbed the delicate petals against her cheek before she sniffed the flower and smiled. "I think you're wrong," she said softly. "And sometime soon you'll discover all the love you deserve."

Damn, he'd never envied a *flower* before. But to caress Eloise's cheek like that was something he wanted to do again. *Soft, warm velvet,* he remembered from last night. "Sure, if you say so," he said, a sense of wanting filling his chest so full he thought he might explode with it.

He forced himself to picture Stevie in that hospital bed and mentally watched all the bills piling up. Three days to go before Crankshank announced who would be promoted. Blake gritted his teeth.

Now was not the time to get distracted.

They searched the acre of morning glories on their knees, lifting vines, peering under the upraised roots of cypress trees, but found nothing that didn't belong. No clues. No scraps of paper that would lead them to the next step in the journey toward wherever the treasure was hidden this year.

He finally told Eloise it was time to go back. The clock was running out. He'd take his licks on this clue, but the next one...

And then he spotted the flag at the front of Crankshank's mansion, whipping in the stiffening breeze until it nearly stood straight out. He squinted, focusing on a tiny white square of paper pinned to one corner of the flag.

A flag rises with the dawn!

From the front porch of the mansion the warning bell sounded. Five minutes until lunch.

Blake broke into a run.

5

IN OBVIOUS FRUSTRATION Blake yanked at the padlock that prevented the flag from being lowered. Instead of a rope that he could have cut with a knife—assuming either he or Eloise had had such a tool—the flag had been raised on a stainless-steel cable that the salt air wouldn't corrode.

"We're going to need a bolt cutter," he said, blowing out a discouraged breath.

"There isn't time." Winded from their run from the far end of the island, Eloise tipped her head back and looked at the flag fluttering in the quickening breeze. It had to be sixty feet to the top of the pole. No way could either of them shinny up there in time to retrieve the clue before lunch was served. Some of the other managers had already gone inside. Blake would receive penalty points.

Unless Eloise could make a small miracle happen.

She wasn't really authorized for that sort of thing. An angel had to be of a much higher rank to call upon such extraordinary powers.

But *this,* Eloise rationalized, was an emergency. And it would only be a teeny, tiny little miracle that would hardly be noticed, she assured herself.

She squinted her eyes closed, drew a deep breath—

"I'll be damned!" Blake said. "The padlock popped open like it was spring-loaded. I must have twisted it just right."

Her eyes flew open. My gracious, she hadn't known she had so much power.

He grinned at her, so full of himself he was about to burst with it. "Come on, let's get that flag down..."

On the piece of paper he retrieved, the next clue read, *Those who can dance may soon advance.*

Their eyes met. He smiled. "There's a room on the second floor the Crankshank ancestors used as a ballroom back in the eighteen hundreds. *This* clue is going to be a snap."

"YOU'RE MAKING no progress at all, Ms. Periwinkle." One cherubic arm folded over the other, Hubert glared at her.

"Blake found his first clue. I admit, we cut it a little short as far as time goes, but he didn't get penalized." Thanks to her wee little miracle, she assumed.

"I meant *progress* in why you are here. By now your quarry should be well and truly in love. Certainly they should feel some attraction for each other." Standing at the kitchen counter, Hubert measured a spoonful of strawberry herbal tea into a pot and added the hot water that had been simmering on the stove.

"They do. I'm sure they do," she lied, giving only fleeting thought to the fact that angels of even the lowest rank shouldn't do that.

But only moments earlier she'd seen what different views they held. As she had slipped out of the dining room following lunch, the entire crew of executives had been discussing ways to convince city councils to loosen overly harsh restrictions on the size of signs, an issue in some communities.

Margaret had thought Blake's method of providing statistics on sales tax growth on well-signed buildings ponderous and a waste of paper. She much preferred supporting selected candidates during elections—and then calling in favors when she needed them. Like Blake, Eloise thought Margaret's technique was just this side of unethical.

"The two of them have done nothing but argue since they sat down for the noon meal," Hubert said. He set the teapot next to a china cup on a wooden tray. Taking a napkin from the cupboard, he folded it into a triangle and placed it and a spoon on the tray.

"That may seem to be the case, but I'm sure—"

"*I'm* sure I need to find a replacement for you, Ms. Periwinkle. This entire experience has confirmed my earlier belief that women are simply not suited to the work my department does."

Eloise felt very much suited for love, which was the business of Hubert's department. She'd simply had some problem getting the two *right* people together.

"If you would replace the darts I lost at the ferry,

I'm confident with even a small dose of the love potion Margaret won't be able to resist Blake.''

"To her eventual regret, I imagine."

"Why would you say that?"

"Mr. Donovan is what you might call a workaholic. He's never had time for romance, and I suspect he would revert to type as soon as the honeymoon was over."

"No, he wouldn't," she said defensively. "Why, he's the most caring man I've ever met. He might be a bit too serious about his work, but that's just because he's under a lot of pressure. He's never had a woman to love, except his mother and sister, of course. It's not fair to judge him if he's never been given a chance."

Hubert arched one pale eyebrow. "I assume your training officer warned you of the dangers of becoming overly fond of your target."

"Yes, of course." She sighed. Clearly that was one warning she should have heeded—obviously a flaw in her character. There'd been other times when she'd become emotionally involved, as she had with the little boy and his puppy. This situation was far more fraught with danger. Her own heart was at risk, and it might be too late to turn back the clock.

Picking up the tea tray, Hubert headed toward the back stairs. "I will expect you to make some progress within the next twenty-four hours or I will be forced to take steps to remedy the situation myself. And don't think for a minute you can call up a miracle or two to accomplish your mission. You are a long way from having been granted that kind of power.''

As she watched him depart, Eloise sternly reminded herself that an angel was *not* supposed to stick out her tongue at anyone—least of all her boss. Besides, if *she* hadn't made that lock open miraculously, who had?

Pondering that question as she returned to the dining room, she found Margaret was the only person still there. Oddly, she was rummaging through the drawers of a huge sideboard, examining every piece of silver she came across. There was a frenetic element to her search, a sense of desperation.

Perfect, Eloise thought. Now if she could get Margaret upstairs to the old ballroom where Blake was searching for his next clue.

"Can I help you find something?" Eloise asked.

Margaret's head came up with a start. Seeing it was Eloise, she visibly relaxed. "Fine by me. Crankshank's little games drive me crazy."

"Blake thinks you thrive on competition."

"Competition I can control." She gave an expansive gesture that managed to take in the entire island. "This is chaos."

Eloise hopped up and sat on the edge of the dining table, letting her feet swing free. In contrast to her own grass-stained dress, Margaret's formfitting slacks were pristine. A man like Blake would surely appreciate a woman who remained so feminine even when dressed in pants.

Considering Margaret's strict, demanding upbringing, Eloise supposed it was reasonable the dear woman never had so much as a single hair out of place. What a strain that must be, to have never had a chance to let down her hair and experience love. Eloise was sure Blake could bring Margaret all the happiness that until now had eluded her.

"I thought Ettienne was partnering with you," Eloise said, trying not to think of the lonely eternity she faced. Particularly if she failed on this assignment. Heaven only knew where she'd be sent next!

"He wasn't much use. Too easily distracted, if you want to know the truth. He kept looking at my boobs instead of where he should have been looking."

"Ah." Eloise nodded in understanding. Human or celestial, it was never easy to be a woman. "So what's the clue you're looking for now?"

The other woman eyed her suspiciously. "Don't you have your own set of clues?"

"Not me. I'm just an observer this time. Too new to be eligible for promotion."

"Well, in that case," she said somewhat reluctantly, "I guess I can use all the help I can get. I'm working on *'A sterling job is its own reward.'*"

"Hmm. Interesting." There ought to be some way Eloise could use that information to lure Margaret upstairs and, hopefully, into Blake's arms.

A tremor of sadness shivered through her. Surely other apprentice cupids were more enthusiastic about the matches they were asked to make. Of course, most of them hadn't shot themselves in the foot with their own damn—er, darn—arrow.

"Have you tried looking upstairs in the ballroom?" Eloise asked, forcing a friendly smile.

Margaret's perfectly smooth forehead pleated into a frown. Her green eyes, artfully enhanced by mascara and eyeliner, narrowed. "No. Should I?"

"I think I saw a big trophy case up there with all kinds of silver cups," she hedged, never having actually seen the inside of the ballroom. "Trophies from sailing regattas, I'd guess. There might be—"

"You are a sweetie! I never would have thought... Where is this ballroom you're talking about?"

"I'll show you."

Leaving the sideboard strewn with the contents of the drawers Margaret had emptied, they hurried out of the room. Eloise's sandals flapped on the hardwood floor; Margaret's three-inch heels made little clicking noises.

"You and Blake seem pretty close," Margaret commented as they mounted the stairs. "Have you two been getting it on?"

Puzzled, Eloise cocked her head. "I've landed on him a couple of times. Accidently. He didn't seem to mind."

Margaret chuckled. "I'd say that would be quite an accident. I've thought about giving him a try myself, just out of curiosity, you understand." They reached the second-floor landing and turned down the hallway. "Is he as good in bed as he looks like he'd be?"

"I'm sure he is." In Eloise's experience, people never did anything particularly *bad* when they were sleeping, except perhaps snore. And they couldn't help that.

The entrance to the ballroom was through an arched double doorway. Noticing a key in the lock, Eloise turned the curved handle, opened the door and stepped into the room. All she had to do was get the two of them together, then nature would no doubt take its course.

Suspicious, Margaret hesitated. Mirrors covered one wall and on the opposite side of the room ceiling-high windows were draped with scarlet velvet, casting the room in the color of fine red wine. Several matching couches were placed strategically around the dance floor, and an old-fashioned Victrola stood alongside a grand piano in one corner of the room. Not a single bit of silver was in sight. Neither was Blake.

"What is this? Some kind of a joke? This place looks like it's been transported right out of a house of ill repute."

"Really?" Eloise glanced around, rather pleased with the combination of bright colors and soft fabrics. "I've never been to a place like that, but I suppose you have. It does seem inviting, doesn't it?"

Margaret's cheeks pinkened and her eyebrows pinched together. "Look, I don't know what you're up to, but it doesn't look to me like there's any trophy cases here." She backed up a step.

"No, don't go." Panicky, Eloise crossed the room to the windows. "I'm sure I saw something. Maybe behind these drapes." She pulled one aside but, of

course, there wasn't anything of use to Margaret behind them. Just windows sealed shut. And she didn't
have a clue where Blake might be.

"You keep looking for me, sweetie. I'm going
back downstairs and finish what I was doing. Let me
know if you find anything."

With that, the door to the ballroom closed.

Eloise ran back across the room. "Wait, Margaret.
I'm sure—"

With a scraping sound, the key turned in the lock.

"Margaret?" Eloise rattled the handle. "What are
you doing? Don't lock me in here." Suddenly aware
of the chilly emptiness of the room, a shiver sped
down her spine. She pounded on the door with her
fist. She remembered another time when celestial children had left her alone, locking her in the chapel because she hadn't known how to play their games.
They'd never wanted her on their teams, had told her
she was a loser. Even though they'd been reprimanded for their misbehavior, she'd always felt—

"Hey, angel, what's wrong?"

She whirled. "Blake!"

To Blake's astonishment, Eloise dashed the length
of the ballroom—her white dress luminous, her curls
bouncing, her expression fearful—and flew into his
arms.

"Where were you?" she sobbed, her small body
trembling. "I thought I was all alone. You weren't
here and Margaret locked the door. I was afraid—"

"Shh, angel, it's all right." He framed her face
with hands that looked overly large against her deli-

cate features. He buried his fingers in her hair and, unable to resist, brushed a kiss across her forehead, a chaste caress of his lips when he really wanted something more. "I was in a game room that's behind this one. I didn't hear you come in. And what's all this about Margaret locking you in?"

"She did. I brought her up here to—" Her eyes widened to bright blue circles. She licked her lips, an intriguing gesture Blake followed with his gaze. "And then she left."

"And now the door's locked."

She nodded, and he could feel her shiver in his arms, though he wasn't entirely sure it was from fear. His masculine ego wanted her reaction to exist for the same reason his stomach was knotted and his slacks were beginning to strain across his groin.

"Let's take a look. Maybe it's just stuck or something."

"I don't think so."

Blake didn't think so, either, once he tried the handle.

"Odd," he announced. At any other time the thought of being locked in the ballroom with Eloise would be decidedly appealing. But not now. Not when the stakes were so high. "We can worry about that later. I'm convinced my next clue is in this room somewhere but I'll be damned if I can find it. I'm glad you're here to help me."

With a tiny frown marring her perfect forehead, she glanced at the door and then back to him. "I'll try. What was the clue again?"

" *'Those who can dance may soon advance.'* " He slid his hands into his pockets, afraid of what he might do if he touched Eloise again. Because he wanted to touch her so much he ached with it. "What do you think it means?" he asked.

"I don't know. I've never learned how to dance."

"You haven't?"

"Where I come from we don't do much of that."

What kind of backwater region did she come from? he wondered. And what man wouldn't be tempted beyond endurance to teach her what she had missed?

"There's a record on that old Victrola in the corner," he said. "I'll give you your first dancing lesson."

"I don't think we should do that." A wariness filled her blue eyes. "Shouldn't we be trying to find your next clue?"

"We are. I'm mean, I think maybe dancing together will trigger the clue," he hedged, recognizing he ought to be backing off, too. "Maybe if we dance around, a trap door will pop up. I don't know."

"Well, if you think it will help…"

Blake didn't know. It just seemed…like maybe he shouldn't examine his motives too closely.

He found the hand crank and wound up the mechanism. The record was an old Bing Crosby tune "True Love," a slow dance Blake could handle even as out of practice as he was. He released the lever and lowered the needle.

"Dancing is like walking in time to the music," he told her. "Just follow what I do."

"I've never been real good at musical things."

"You'll do fine. I promise."

The record was scratchy, the crooner from another, gentler era, the lyrics sentimental.

Enchanted by Eloise's look of intense concentration, Blake placed his hand at her waist and took her hand in his. But he didn't pull her close. That would really be courting trouble. "Relax," he whispered.

Relax? Eloise didn't imagine that was possible with Blake holding her, even so stiffly. His shoulder flexed beneath her hand; the heat of his palm permeated the fabric of her dress to sear the small of her back. Dimly she was aware of the music, a heavenly melody, as Blake glided her around the room. Instinctively, their bodies moved together, at first hesitantly, and then—as if almost unwillingly—in perfect rhythm.

She caught their reflection in the wall of mirrors, their images floating as though they were dancing on a scarlet-colored cloud. Her skirt flared and twirled in a white billow of air. He dipped her, his strong arms holding her safely as though she weighed nothing at all.

This is wrong! a small voice of conscience warned her. *She* wasn't the one who belonged in Blake's arms.

The music came to a stop. Their eyes met. Eloise's heart beat wildly, as though she had run for miles, and air crowded her lungs. Then his gaze, as dark as midnight, shifted to her lips.

"I don't know what's gotten into me," he whispered, his voice low and intimate. Slanting his head slightly, his mouth covered hers.

Eloise knew the answer. Even so, she couldn't find the strength to stop him.

The press of his lips brought with it a glimpse of paradise, a pure joyous feeling of coming home. Celestial bells chimed. A heavenly choir sang a hallelujah chorus. His tongue slid along the seam of her lips in search of a way in, and she willingly gave him entry. Shocking pleasure shot through her.

She had never imagined a kiss could be so exciting.

Both the dance and Blake's kiss felt so very right. But it was wrong, the insistent voice of reason warned. An illusion created by Cupid's errant arrow Eloise had impaled in her own foot.

Blake lifted his head. "What was that? Did you hear something?"

All she could hear was the heavy beat of her heart pulsing through her body and the raspy noise of the record that had reached the end of the song—accompanied by the discordant clamor of her conscience.

"I...didn't hear anything." Her voice felt thick in her throat.

"Wait a minute."

He left her standing there, her knees rubbery, her body weak with a wanting she couldn't quite define and didn't dare acknowledge.

He lifted the arm on the record player and placed it down again.

The last notes of the song carried through the empty room. The needle screeched into a new groove.

"A superior swimmer could be the winner." A man's voice, tinny and shallow, repeated the clue that had been recorded at the end of the song. Finally the voice added the warning, "You must find the next clue while the sun is still up."

Blake grinned. "We found it, angel! No problem!" He crossed the room, lifted her off her feet and spun her around, laughing. "I think I love you, sweetheart. This is the best I've ever done. Two out of two right off the bat. This one was easy, huh?"

Eloise caught her breath. *Easy?* She had the terrible premonition the price had been losing her heart.

"Of course, that doesn't mean this next one about swimmers won't stump us," he said.

"So far, so good," she responded distractedly. There was more on her mind at the moment than Crankshank's clues—the thrumming heat that was melting her from the inside out, the pulsing warmth still on her lips, the taste of Blake on her tongue.

"There's a heck of a lot of water around here. Hard to know where to start. The swimming beach is the most obvious place." He released her, brushing her hair away from her face with the back of his hand.

"Yes," she whispered, mesmerized by his gentle touch. He'd made his declaration of love lightly, as though he didn't quite believe it himself. But Eloise did, and that made her situation desperate—because she was falling in love, too. She had to do something and do it quickly to prevent a disaster from happening.

Only three days remained, and Margaret and Blake

wouldn't see each other for another year. Time was quickly running out.

An *antidote,* she thought, glancing frantically around the room at the velvet curtains, the glossy dance floor where Blake had held her in his arms, and the mirrors where she'd seen them together. People fell in and out of love every day. Even she knew that much about the human condition. There had to be something that reversed Cupid's potion. There *had* to be.

If she didn't find a way to reverse the spinning tide of emotion, Blake would be hurt. It didn't bear thinking about how she would survive experiencing love and then losing it. An eternity in heaven without him would seem like hell.

Across the room, the key turned with a click in the lock.

"Hey, you two love birds." Terry poked his head in through the open door. "Margaret said you were up here. You gotta come see. Ettienne has found some of the *real* Crankshank treasure. The *pirate's* buried treasure. He's found an 1810 gold doubloon."

6

"I TELL YOU, there's a fortune on this island."

Everyone had gathered around Ettienne in the middle of the parlor room. Straining to look over Spencer's shoulder, Blake caught sight of the gold doubloon in Ettienne's palm. It shone there, tempting and within easy reach. He wondered how much it would be worth compared to the bonus riding on the outcome of Crankshank's corporate treasure hunt. And if it were really possible to find more coins on the island.

"How do you know it's real?" Blake asked.

"I know gold when I see it," Ettienne insisted. "This is the real McCoy, and there's sure to be more where this came from. Probably a whole treasure chest full of 'em."

"Where'd you find it?" the regional manager from New Mexico asked.

"Was it buried, or just lying there?" someone else asked before Ettienne had a chance to answer the first question.

Blake backed away from the press of his co-workers, who were firing one question after another at Ettienne. He'd been shaken by his reaction to Eloise upstairs in the ballroom, the powerful emotions that had flared through him with Eloise in his arms.

And then reality had intruded with the arrival of Terry at the door. Thankfully, Blake had come to his senses. Or so he told himself. For Stevie's sake, he had to keep his priorities straight.

"Come on, you guys," Ettienne shouted over the noise of the crowd. "Let's get out there and find the rest of the treasure. We'll all be rich. Then ol' Crankshank can take his job and his promotion and his stupid games and stuff them where—"

"Be careful, Ettienne," Margaret cautioned. "You don't want to have to eat those words."

He waved her warning off with a shake of his head. "I'm going to find that treasure, Crankshank be damned. Anybody who wants can come with me. Equal shares."

He shoved his way through the crowd, followed by four or five regional directors.

"I saw a shovel in the toolshed," Terry told them. "I'll get that."

"What we need is a metal detector," another man said, pushing his way to the door.

"There's a storm coming tonight," Ettienne shouted over his shoulder. "We'll have to hurry."

"You're making a mistake, gentlemen," Spencer called after the departing figures. "If that treasure had been easy to find, assuming it actually exists, it would have been located years ago. Don't waste your time."

A horde of heavy footsteps shook the front hallway; the screen door to the porch banged shut.

As far as Blake could tell, Spencer's wise counsel fell on deaf ears. The mass exodus left only five of them in the room—Spencer, Margaret, the young regional director from Iowa whose name Blake had trouble remembering, himself and Eloise. She'd been hanging back at the fringes of the group, which was just as well because she might have been trampled if she'd gotten in their way.

Margaret turned toward those still remaining in the room, smiling slightly. "Looks like that diversion narrowed the competition."

"Hey, you didn't plant that doubloon, did you?" Blake asked suspiciously.

Her smile was all innocence and probably phony as hell. "If I know Crankshank, I didn't need to. He's probably up to his usual tricks."

Outside, Terry's voice rose above the rest. "If I'm going to do all the digging, I get more than one share."

"No way, man," someone responded as the argument faded into the distance.

Spencer said, "Why they've allowed themselves to be distracted is less important than what we do now. I suggest the five of us work together. That way we'll be able to accomplish more than if we struggle on alone."

"Fine by me," the kid from Iowa said.

"Good, Bob, I'm glad to have you on my team," Spencer agreed. He glanced toward Margaret. "I'd be glad to work with you, too."

"Neither one of you has found your first two

clues," she said. "If I team up with you, I'll be losing ground. I'd rather work solo, thanks."

Eloise said, "Did you find the silver clue?"

"You bet," Margaret replied. "In fact you were right about the trophy case, except it was in the hallway. We've been walking past it every time we went in to eat, and it totally slipped my mind. I owe you."

Darting a glance at Blake, Eloise shrugged. "Glad I could help."

For the life of him, Blake didn't understand why Eloise was so eager to help Margaret. He resented it. Damn it all, didn't she know *they* were a team?

"So what about you two?" Spencer asked Blake and Eloise. "Want to throw in with us?"

Blake shoved his hands into his pockets. "Truth is, I'm tempted to go with the rest of them. If those doubloons are for real—"

"They're not," Margaret insisted.

"I agree it's unlikely," Blake said. "And I really need that promotion, folks. So, since Eloise and I are getting along pretty good with just the two of us, I think I'll stick with what's working. But thanks for asking."

"*Need* the promotion?" Spencer asked, eyebrows raised as he locked onto Blake's slip of the tongue. "Is there a problem?"

"Nothing I can't work out," Blake assured him with more confidence than he actually felt. And he sure didn't want to blab his troubles in front of Margaret, who wasn't exactly the sympathetic type.

"Very well, if we're all set on our course..." Spencer waited until Eloise nodded her agreement, then looped his arm around Bob's shoulder. "Come on, young man. Looks like we've got our work cut out for us. I'll tell you about some of the tricks I've learned over the years. Crankshank is no fool when he plans these little treasure hunts. It's the very devil to solve his riddles but it sure hones your creativity. I have my suspicions he's set us up again for one of those knock-down, drag-out battles. It's a wonder this old place is still standing."

The pair left, and Blake figured the youngster would probably learn a lot from the older man. But it was unlikely they would win the game. He—and Margaret—were still in the driver's seat.

"Spencer seems to get a charge out of Crankshank's games every year," Margaret said. "Frankly, I could do without them. Thank goodness he's not here this year. The smell of that awful syrupy strawberry tea he drinks makes me sick to my stomach. At least I can concentrate on something besides not throwing up."

"Right." Blake checked his watch. "We've got a couple of hours before dinner. Time enough to track down the next clue, I'd say."

"I'm on my way." Pulling a slip of paper from her pocket, Margaret smiled. "Hope you won't mind if I wish you bad luck. I'd really like that promotion, too."

"You'll have to go through me to get it," Blake promised.

"I never doubted it for a moment." With that, Margaret left the room. A moment later the front door closed behind her.

The sudden silence in the house crackled with Blake's awareness that he was alone with Eloise again. Wanted to kiss her again. And wouldn't dare be distracted again.

"Do any of the sales directors drink strawberry herbal tea?" she asked.

That question stopped him. He'd been thinking about kissing—and more—and she'd been thinking about tea? Talk about being on different pages of the play book. "We're mostly coffee drinkers, I think. Crankshank is the only one I know who drinks that sissy stuff."

"Oh." Cute little furrows pleated her forehead.

"Why d'you ask?"

"It's nothing really. Only that I saw Hubert fussing with some strawberry tea. I thought maybe—"

"Trust me, if Obadiah were around, we'd know it. He loves to watch us make fools of ourselves over his games."

"I'm sure you're right." She lifted her shoulders apologetically. "So what do we do next?"

How 'bout we go upstairs and I make mad, passionate love to you?

By force of will, Blake cleared the thought from his mind and the interesting images it conjured in his imagination. Checking his watch, he realized half the afternoon was gone. Invariably he lost track of time when Eloise was around. "Guess we need to take off our dancing shoes and put on our swim trunks. The clue said swimmers are winners.''

''Swim trunks?''

''You did bring a swimsuit with you, didn't you?''

''I'll, uh, have to check.'' Eloise didn't exactly know the full extent of the wardrobe Hubert had provided. She'd simply taken things out of the closet or chest of drawers as she'd needed them.

With a nod, she went upstairs with Blake.

The moment she heard him in his own room—changing clothes, she presumed—she ducked out of her room and hurried to Hubert's quarters.

She desperately needed something from the senior cupid-turned-butler, and it wasn't a swimsuit but the antidote to love. From the look she'd seen in Blake's eyes—and felt echoed in her own heart—things could get out of hand if she didn't find it soon.

She found him in his room, his legs propped on a footstool, munching on a tray of gooey desserts, and watching a girlie show on a big-screen television.

''Hubert! Whatever are you—''

He snapped off the image with the flick of his hand. ''Understanding earthly temptation is all part of the job, my dear.''

Yeah, right! ''Look, Hubert, if you aren't going to give me any more darts, you need to give me an antidote for the potion that was on the tips of those arrows.''

His pale eyebrows rose. ''What makes you think there is one?''

''There has to be. People fall *out* of love almost as

often as they fall *in* love. There has to be some reason."

"That human foible is certainly not the fault of *my* department. Once they've been struck by one of our arrows, they're on their own."

"But there has to be something."

"You could try poison, I suppose."

Good heavens! Eloise wouldn't do that. She'd far rather give up her own brief time on earth than risk Blake's life.

"My dear girl, don't you know falling out of love has more to do with boredom, or losing trust in one another, than it does with any magic?"

"No, I guess I didn't know that." How could she, since this was the only time she'd experienced the emotion firsthand? And she couldn't imagine not always being enthralled by Blake, or not trusting in his feelings for her. Assuming he loved her back, of course. But she supposed she lacked any real basis on which to judge his interest in her.

"If you find something that works, my dear, do let me know. I've seen a lot of wives who'd be happy to give their husbands a big dose of an antidote when they've fallen for the 'other' woman."

"I'll keep that in mind." From the beginning, Hubert hadn't been the least bit of help to Eloise. He seemed determined to see her fail. That meant he could be lying to her now, so she'd have to keep looking for an antidote on her own.

She turned to leave, then had a second thought.

"Would you like me to bring you a cup of strawberry tea while you're watching television?"

"Mercy, no." He snapped the TV back on and quickly changed the channel to a program about alligators in the Australian outback. "I much prefer lemon tea over that dreadfully sweet brew. But there's no need to bring me any. I had a pot with my noon meal." With a negligent wave of his hand, he gestured toward the tray that sat on the table beside his comfortable chair.

It was just as well Hubert hadn't taken Eloise up on her offer. She had to hurry back upstairs and change into her swimsuit. But Hubert's dislike of strawberry tea did give her pause. If he hadn't been brewing a pot for himself, who had he been making it for?

"THIS IS THE ONLY swimming beach on the island," Blake explained as Eloise shrugged out of her cotton cover-up.

She shivered slightly and hugged herself. The suit she'd found in her room was far too revealing to be angelic. She had more bare skin showing than any cupid had a right. To her dismay, Blake perused every square inch of her flesh, his gaze cruising with lingering persistence from the top of her head to the tips of her toes, making them curl into the sand. Heat flared in her cheeks.

Those who did not harbor sinful thoughts had no reason to blush, she recalled hearing somewhere.

Shoot, it ought to be Blake who was blushing. She

had a pretty darn good idea what he was thinking.
The problem was, growing overly at home in her human form, she was thinking about it, too.

"The water looks refreshing," she managed to say,
though in reality it looked cold, dark and dangerous,
the waves no longer lapping benignly at the shore but
rolling up to the beach in an angry foamy froth. In
the distance, dark clouds had gathered on the horizon.

"Let's see what we can find. The next clue has to
be here somewhere." Turning, Blake dropped his
towel to the sand and waded toward the breakers. A
whole ocean of cold water was exactly what he
needed. That had to be the skimpiest white swimsuit—on the best-looking body—he'd ever seen.

Trying to chill out, and chill down, he kept on
walking. Ducking, he let a wave crash over him.
When he bobbed to the surface, he heard a scream.

"Bla...ake!"

Treading water, he spun around.

It was Eloise, her head breaking water for only an
instant before she sank out of sight. Her arms reappeared, beating the water as though she was being
attacked by a swarm of biting flies. Or sharks.

"Damn!" Obviously she didn't know any more
about swimming than she had about dancing. So why
the hell had she followed him into the waves? Why
hadn't she said something?

Lunging forward, he stroked his way toward her as
the wave receded. A moment later he was standing
waist-deep in water. He reached down to pluck her
from beneath the surface.

She came up sputtering and coughing. "Dear heavenly days! For all you noticed, I could have been dead!"

"All you had to do was put your feet down, angel. It's shallow here."

With an angry swipe of her hand, she shoved the hair out of her face. "*Shallow?* I'll tell you about shallow. That wave knocked me off my feet, dragged me halfway to Ireland and then spat me back out. I could have drowned," she wailed, "and you're talking *shallow?*"

His lips twitched as he valiantly tried to repress a smile. He loved her intensity—the fury, the outrage in her cornflower blue eyes. And he loved the cool velvety feel of her skin beneath his hands. Urges stirred that no amount of frigid water or the lure of a bonus could dampen.

"You should have told me you don't know how to swim," he said softly without reproach.

Another wave came, the foam whizzing past them, the force of the water shifting their feet in the sand. She clamped onto his biceps and held on tight, her eyes widening even farther as her fingers dug in. He slipped his arms around her waist. Her generous breasts pressed against his chest, his untamed arousal making itself known against her abdomen.

"I'll keep you safe," he promised. *Forever,* he wanted to add, but some small voice of reason held him back. He'd known Eloise for less than twenty-four hours. What he was feeling could be nothing more than a fluke, an anomaly in an otherwise rational world. Before he'd met her, he'd never even conceded that the power of love existed; he'd seen the damage that fantasy had done to others.

"I don't think I want to go swimming," she said, her big eyes filling with tears. "I'm sorry about the clue. I know you need to find—"

"It's okay." Lifting her to cradle her in his arms, he walked out of the water. He wanted to keep right on walking, all the way up to his room, to the big canopied bed, but instead he lowered her to her feet. He picked up a towel and dried her hair, then her shoulders.

With the lightest touch, like the wings of a firefly, her fingertips caressed his chest. "It's soft," she whispered.

He nearly gasped aloud. "What's soft?"

"The hair on your chest. Like black silk. I wondered last night."

Certain other parts of his anatomy were anything but soft. He clamped his teeth together to prevent a groan from escaping. God, couldn't she tell what she was doing to him? Not that he wanted her to stop. But this was a public beach.

Those same delicate fingertips wandered to his face, caressed his cheek and explored the cleft in his chin.

"Did you know you have a dimple?" she asked, her eyes filled with curiosity. "Right there," she said, resting her finger on the slight indentation.

"Yeah, I've noticed." His voice was raspy and rough, his legs none too steady. "When I shave."

"I suppose I shouldn't..." Her finger crept up to cover his lips, silencing his voice but not the pounding of his heart or the roar of the ocean behind him, the rising tide licking at the spot where they were standing. "I liked kissing you."

"The feeling is definitely mutual." Her admission pleased him more than he could say.

She smiled the sweetest, most seductive smile he'd ever seen. Hell, he was ahead of everybody else on the clues. Why should he fight the feeling?

"I'm glad."

Circling her with the towel, he brought her closer. With her smile still beatific, she lifted her face for his kiss, an invitation he couldn't resist. Blake closed his mouth over hers.

As he tasted her, a wave swept up the beach reaching him calf high and dragging a bit of seaweed across his ankle. But Eloise's flavor was sweet, warm honey. No power on earth could dampen his ardor.

The seaweed brushed against him again. Unwilling to let go of Eloise, he tried to step away from the twining seaweed, but the tentacle clung to him, this time wrapping itself around his ankle. As the wave receded, the octopus-like arm tugged him toward deeper water.

"What the hell!" Releasing Eloise, he looked down at his foot.

He'd been snared by a heavy fishing line, not seaweed, and each time he raised his foot, the line moved. He reached down, untangled himself and gave the line a yank.

"What are you doing?" Eloise asked.

"I'm not sure."

The line had been buried. It rose up out of the dry sand and extended out into the ocean. Wrapping the line around his hand, Blake pulled whatever was out there toward him.

Terry came jogging down the beach, his pants rolled up to his knees, his feet bare.

"Jeez, you two. How can you go fishing at a time like this? We've discovered a cave at the south end of the island near where Ettienne found the doubloon." Without breaking his stride, or breaking into a sweat, Terry jogged past them. "The entrance has collapsed but we think the treasure might be inside there somewhere."

"Be careful," Blake warned, halting his efforts for the moment. He'd retrieve whatever was in the water after Terry was out of sight. "Cave-ins can be dangerous." And Blake had little doubt that this one had probably been arranged by Crankshank for some purpose of his own.

"We know." Terry gave an unconcerned wave over his shoulder. "I'm going for some wood to shore up the walls. You ought to get in on the deal while you still can."

Blake wasn't interested. But he was damn curious about what was at the end of his fishing line. He began reeling it in again.

"Shouldn't we stop them?" Eloise asked, watching Terry as he turned inland on his jog from the beach.

"With the storm coming, a cave could fill with water. They could all drown."

"I don't think that's very likely. Besides…" He grunted as a slender leather briefcase flopped onto the beach like a dead fish at the end of his line. "I think we've found our next clue." And long before the deadline of the setting sun, too. Just as well since a storm was brewing.

"Oh, my gracious!" she cried.

She knelt beside him as he opened the case, their thighs brushing, the hair on his legs rough against her velvety smoothness. Damn, how could he even think about Crankshank's clues when she was so close? How could he not when Stevie's future was at stake?

The snap released easily enough. Inside the case he found a piece of paper sealed in plastic.

Promotion may come to those who enjoy the right motion.

"Damn!" he muttered, sitting back on his haunches.

"What's the matter?"

"You figure out one of Crankshank's stupid riddles and all you get is the next one. I feel like I'm treading water. Maybe I ought to forget the whole damn thing and link up with Terry. Searching for buried treasure has got to be easier than this."

She palmed his cheek, her hand warm against his afternoon whiskers. "You're not a quitter, Blake. We'll figure this clue out, just like we have the others."

Faith blazed in her eyes like blue fire, so powerful

Blake would have rather walked on water than fail her. "Okay, let's put our heads together." And our lips, our bodies, whatever she'd let him. "Where do we start with this one?"

Still squatting on the sand, she turned toward the Crankshank mansion, a huge gray mausoleum towering over the entire island. She squinted, shading her eyes with her hand against the afternoon sun.

"Isn't everyone at the cave or hunting for their own clues somewhere out here on the island?" she asked.

He shrugged. "So far as I know, they are."

"I could have sworn I saw a curtain move in that third-floor window, the one right below the widow's walk."

Following the direction of her gaze, he scrutinized the top row of windows. Nothing moved that he could see. "It was probably just an open window and the wind blowing the curtains." He levered himself upright, bringing Eloise to her feet with him. The breeze had already dried her hair, and her silver-blond curls danced around her head. He envied them the freedom of their caress.

He let his gaze slide across the length of the house. Behind it, protected from Atlantic storms for a century or more, a huge oak tree stretched it limbs. It shouldn't have been there but it was, an affirmation of endurance against all odds.

And from one of its biggest branches, Blake remembered, dangled an old tire swing, a swing probably dozens of little Crankshanks had enjoyed over the years. Hanging suspended by three sturdy chains, more than one child could play on the swing at once.

"How would you like to go for a swing?" he asked Eloise. "Are you game?"

She looked at him oddly. "I've been swinging from stars for as long as I can remember."

"Good. Because I think I know where our next clue is." He took her hand and pulled her along at a dead run. He felt free and good, competent to solve any problem. He was more alive than he had been in years.

He could do this. He could win everything.

Eloise somehow managed to give him a supernatural sense that he would succeed at anything he tried.

7

"I'M DIZZY," Eloise cried, laughing. The island whirled around her in a blur as Blake spun the tire swing. He sat opposite her, their knees alternating one with the other in the center of the circle. Above her, the heavy chain supporting the swing creaked and groaned where the three sections came together, tugging at the massive branch of the oak tree.

"Concentrate on me," Blake told her. "That way you won't get woozy."

"That's what I'm doing." Breathless, she looked into his gray eyes, seeing the sparkle of a mischievous boy there, replacing the usual glimmer of darkness she'd observed. She watched his dark hair riffle in the wind, relished his easy, relaxed smile. The combination of everything she saw and felt made her dizzy with love.

Throughout the universe, Cupid's magic potion was known as the most potent of all forces. She must have gotten a double dose.

"We probably shouldn't be doing this. It feels too much like fun." His grin broadened and he set the swing on a looping course.

She gasped as much from joy as the breath-stealing motion. "You're right." In her celestial world she'd often felt out of place, as though everyone belonged there except her. She'd endured an eternity of lonely days. And nights. "But we're supposed to be looking for the next clue," she reminded him.

"We are. Sort of."

This was an impossible situation, one that was temporary at best—and very likely disastrous to both her future and his. It should be another woman experiencing this heady sensation with Blake. Not Eloise.

Her throat nearly closed around that wretched thought, and she fought to remember why she was here. "It's almost dinnertime. If you don't find the clue—"

"I'll get penalty points. I know." He lowered his foot to the ground to slow the spinning swing. Little by little the island came back into focus. "I remember taking my kid sister to the park when she was about three. Our old man had already taken off by then. Mom was working full-time and I was baby-sitting Caroline after school."

"You must have been pretty young yourself."

"Eight or nine, I suppose. Young enough to resent that I couldn't go play with the guys. And then I saw a father bringing his kid into the park—you know, a toddler, I guess you call 'em—riding up on his shoulders. And I couldn't ever remember my dad doing that for me. And he sure as hell wasn't around for Caroline that way." He looked off into the distance toward the mainland, though Eloise suspected he was actually seeing his past, the one she'd read about. "I swore then if I ever got to be a father I'd take my kid to the park every damn chance I could. And it would be a park where the kids weren't carrying guns or selling dope.''

Emotion welled in Eloise's chest, filling her until she could barely breathe. ''You'd make a wonderful father.'' She'd love to see a softer version of his rugged features on the face of an infant, capped by his dark hair, the echo of his eyes gazing up at her. Maybe when she was transferred out of Cupid's Celestial Division—and she was sure she would be if Hubert had his way—she'd plead for a second chance in the Baby Department. She'd look for a baby like that to send to Blake and his—

Tears burned in her eyes and her stomach knotted at the sudden realization. Damn—darn it all! *She* wanted to be the woman to carry Blake's child in her womb, hold him in her arms and keep him safe until it was time for him to explore the outer reaches of space. And she'd never, ever have the chance.

Her vision blurred. She climbed out of the swing and ran, stumbling, toward the Crankshank mansion. She'd had no idea love could be such a painful emotion. Why on earth would heaven wish such a terrible ordeal on anyone?

''Wait, Eloise!'' The swing squeaked as he got off to follow her. ''What's wrong?''

Without looking back, she waved him to stay away. This was one time when she needed to be alone.

SHE WAS LATE to dinner.

After returning to the mansion, Eloise had searched

through every shelf in the storeroom, rearranged every box, can and jar, in the hope of finding the antidote she needed. She'd found her way down to the basement. Brushing aside curtains of spider webs, she'd rummaged through old cans of paint. The weed killer she'd found had given her the shivers. Poison most certainly wasn't the answer.

Now, with everyone else in the dining room, she could check the upstairs bathrooms' medicine cabinets.

In the third bathroom she tried, she yanked open the cabinet door. Pill bottles spilled out, clattering into the sink. Hurriedly she checked the labels. Except that they were prescriptions for Obadiah Crankshank, they could have been written in Greek for all the information they gave her.

She swiped at the remaining bottles on the shelves. A mouthwash. Aspirin. And one single brown bottle with a stopper. The label read Universal Antidote.

"Thank heaven!" she cried, nearly in tears again, this time with relief. The bottle looked old, the label faded. She didn't know if the concoction was an antidote for snake bite, poison, or love. But it said *universal* so that made it worth trying.

Snatching the bottle from the shelf, she raced out of the room and downstairs. As she reached the dining room, she tucked it in her skirt pocket, drew a calming breath and found the seat Blake had saved for her.

"Are you all right?" he whispered, half standing to help her with her chair. Hubert had already served the soup course, and the others were enjoying their meal, the conversation subdued.

"Fine," she said, taking the napkin from her place and spreading it across her lap. Hubert appeared, as if by magic, with her bowl of soup.

After the butler stepped out of hearing distance, Blake said, "When you ran off, I got worried. And then I couldn't find you…"

"I'm fine. Really." She smiled tautly across the table at Margaret, who eyed her curiously. Eloise couldn't help wondering—and hating the thought— that someday Blake's baby would belong to the strikingly attractive woman. It was hard to imagine Margaret heavy with child. It simply wasn't her style.

But then, love had the power to change a woman, or so she'd heard.

Using her spoon, Eloise sipped the soup, and found it hard to swallow even a small taste of the rich, flavorful broth. Her emotions were simply running too high. Somehow, for her sake as well as Blake's, she had to find a way to slip the antidote into his food. She'd have to wait until everyone at the table was distracted, then do the deed when no one was watching.

From the head of the table, which Spencer had appropriated in Crankshank's absence to give himself and his girth more room, he asked Blake, "So how are you doing with your clues?"

"I'm on top of them," Blake responded. "Eloise has been a lot of help. How 'bout you and Bob?"

"Unfortunately we missed one this afternoon."

Spencer shrugged; Bob looked embarrassed. "But I learned that Bob is the head of Des Moines Tomorrow, a chamber of commerce committee that's doing dynamite things for the city. We might not have found the clue we were looking for but I sure as hell learned a lot from him."

"That's great." Blake nodded his approval. He'd done some work with the local chamber, too. In fact, years ago Spencer had been the one to suggest he get more active in the community. It had paid off in both sales and connections. Heck, he'd even sold a big electronic billboard because he'd done some coaching for his nephew's Little League team, though that hadn't been Blake's motive for helping out.

All eyes swung toward Margaret.

She smiled smugly. "No penalty points for me."

"So far," Blake mumbled under his breath.

"You folks are missing a sure thing," Terry said as Hubert removed his soup bowl and replaced it with a dinner plate. "We've found a tunnel at the back of that cave at the south end of the island. We figure that's where the old Crankshank pirate buried his treasure."

Ettienne piped up. "It could also be a tunnel the pirate planned to use to escape if he was attacked. It probably runs all the way to the house."

"Tomorrow we're going to dig through to wherever it begins," Terry said. "I'll bet dollars to donuts there's a pile of gold at the source. In fact, I bet that's why Crankshank puts us through this ordeal every year. He wants the treasure found as much as we do."

"More likely you'll be undermining the house or digging him a free basement," Spencer warned. "You'd be better off sticking with why we're here—to make Crest Enterprises the biggest and best sign maker in the world."

"You're exaggerating, Spencer," Terry said. "We only operate in North America. Not the world."

"Yet!" Spencer responded, chuckling and smiling good-naturedly.

There was a lot of mumbling and disagreeing among the executives. Eloise used that opportunity to sprinkle half the contents of the brown bottle on Blake's seafood linguini and the rest on her own dinner. The taste was a little salty but not unpleasantly so. She could only hope the results were what she intended.

She held her breath as she forced down a second bite; there was no detectable change in her feelings for Blake. None at all.

He still looked devastatingly handsome, his nose straight and regal, his jaw square and determined, his dark brows nicely arched. He was wearing a sport shirt open at the collar and a tuft of his silken chest hair was visible at the vee. Eloise's fingers itched to feel that fine texture again.

He cast her a sidelong glance. "I found the next clue. It was stuck inside the tire."

"I'm glad." Maybe the antidote took a while to work. There was still an intensity in Blake's eyes, and a softening around his sensual mouth that jolted Eloise's heart. Her insides warmed in response.

"'*A single in the dark should be careful not to trip over a shingle.*'"

She looked at him blankly. No one else at the table seemed to be interested in what they were saying. The argument over which treasure to pursue was much too loud and impassioned for the other managers to give her conversation with Blake any heed.

"That's the clue," Blake said when she didn't respond. "I figure the next one's somewhere on the roof."

"Blake, we can't go climbing around on the roof in the middle of the night. The house has three stories, *plus* a widow's walk."

"Are you afraid of heights?"

"Well, no." Accustomed to peering down from a pinnacle of clouds, height was no problem for Eloise. "But I'm not eager to break my neck, either." Not that she thought she could die, precisely. But she could do some painful damage to her human body.

"If you feel that way, maybe I should ask Margaret if she would like to help me out." His lips canted into a teasing grin.

All the blood drained from Eloise's face. Dear heaven! The antidote was working. "Yes, I think that's a good—"

"Hey, angel, I was just kidding." He took her hand under the table and gently squeezed her fingers. "I'm not about to go anywhere with Margaret. You know that."

In spite of herself, Eloise squeezed back. Her chin

trembled. "She's lots smarter than I am. And prettier, too."

"Not the way I look at things."

No one had ever thought Eloise had an ounce of intelligence; she'd bungled her way through every assignment she'd been given. Certainly no one had ever said she was pretty. Love must indeed be blind, she concluded. But her heart leaped at the knowledge that Blake was the one individual in the entire universe who disagreed with the majority opinion.

She watched in wonder and regret as he turned from her to consume every last bite of linguini on his plate. If the antidote was going to work, it would be soon.

IT TOOK Blake a while to locate a flashlight. It was several minutes more before he found Eloise, who'd fled into the parlor room with the others after dinner. She was his lucky charm, his talisman, the reason the clues were coming to him so easily at this retreat when in the past he'd struggled. Thank goodness she'd come along this year when the outcome was so critical.

She was standing at the back of the room away from the others. He slipped up behind her and slid his arm around her waist.

She jumped. "Blake!" she whispered. "What are you doing?"

"I've got a flashlight. Let's go."

"Don't you want to hear Spencer discuss the new tubular plastic technology the company's using?"

"Not a chance. I want to go hang out in dark places with you."

Eloise shot a fleeting glance toward the roomful of people. If she could just catch Margaret's eye maybe there'd still be a chance—

But it was no use.

Blake was far too determined to get her, not Margaret, alone. And if she were honest with herself, Eloise wanted that, too.

Obviously the antidote had been a flop and something less than *universal*. She could only hope no one got a snake bite and needed the same medicine.

By the time they reached the third floor and the ladder to the widow's walk, Eloise was slightly out of breath. Blake climbed up first, shoving open the trapdoor. He turned to assist her, helping her into a small window-lined room. It smelled a bit musty, as though no one had been up here in a very long time. The covering over a narrow cot by the wall was tattered, the dust on a small desk inches deep.

The door opened easily to the exterior walkway that encircled the chamber. Wives of seafaring men— or pirates on the lookout—had stood at this lofty place gazing out to sea.

Shaking her head, and filled with doubts about the wisdom of Blake's decision to explore the roof at night, Eloise followed him outside. She left the door standing ajar.

The evening was dark, clouds obscuring the stars, and a brisk wind was blowing in from the ocean. Eloise hugged herself as much from the cool air as from the hum of anticipation that thrummed through her body.

"I should have thought to get you a sweater," Blake said, placing a warming arm around her shoulders. "But if we can spot the next clue, we won't be up here long."

Clicking on the flashlight, he skimmed the column of light across the steeply sloping roof. The shingles were old and weathered; a collection of vents protruded at random, and on the north side of the big brick chimney there was a slippery covering of moss. The odd array of cupolas gave the roofline a jigsaw effect.

"Blake, we can't find anything in the pitch black. Let's go back and try again in the morning."

"The clue said something about tripping over a shingle in the dark. I figure we're looking for something that glows in the dark and we'd never be able to see it in the daylight."

Though his logic seemed impeccable, Eloise had a bad feeling about this. She'd had a similar bad feeling when a guardian angel she knew had been inattentive in watching over John Bobbitt. And look what Lorena had done then...

"I'm not so sure..." she began.

But Blake had already left her side, crossing to the edge of the platform and stepping over the low wrought-iron railing. "The shingles are flat across the roof peak," he said. "About six inches wide. We can walk along that. Come on." He extended his hand. "I won't let you fall."

"Shouldn't we have a safety rope or something?"

He grinned at her, a flash of white teeth in the darkness. "Hey, my job when I started with Crest was installing signs, some of them on skyscrapers. Crankshank hired me himself when Crest had no more than a hundred employees. They called me Sure-Footed Donovan. We'll be fine."

Eloise wasn't quite so confident as she peered across the roof's expanse. "I once knew a tightrope walker who developed an inner ear infection and lost his balance."

"What happened?"

"He fell."

"To his death?"

"Oh, no." In one of her more successful efforts, she'd edged a bunch of clowns underneath the wire and they'd broken his fall with all of their balloons. "But he did have to give up his job. He's in the demolition business now. You know, blowing up buildings."

"Oh, that sounds much safer," Blake said dryly. He offered her his hand.

She'd been reassigned after that. It seemed no one believed she could handle being around all that TNT without blowing heaven knew what up.

Gingerly, she hiked up her skirt and stepped over the railing. His hand closed around hers, warm and strong and ever so confident.

"Maybe we'll come back up here in the daylight just for the view," he told her.

They edged forward along the endless roof, the

light bouncing across the shingles. Below them, the waves rolled against the beach in a steady drone. Lights on the mainland twinkled like tiny fireflies.

Eloise's foot slipped.

"Oh, my gosh!"

Blake steadied her. "You're okay. I've got you."

"I really don't think this is a good idea, Blake. Let's go back."

A gust of wind caught her skirt. A door slammed behind her. She turned quickly to see what had happened.

That was a big mistake.

Her hasty movement caused her to lose her already precarious balance. Her arms flailed; she grabbed at air. And her feet went out from under her.

"Bla...a...a...ke!" she screamed.

She slid down the roof. Shingles crackled and splintered. She dug her fingers into the wood but couldn't find any purchase. In slow motion, her unstoppable descent continued.

"Grab something!" Blake shouted.

"I'm trying," she mumbled, struggling so hard to cling to anything in her path that she didn't have time to yell back.

"To your right. There's a vent. Grab it!"

Easier said than done. But she tried to crab-crawl her fall that direction. The vent appeared in her line of sight. Then slowly slipped on—

She snared it. Barely. With her fingertips. But enough so she could haul herself closer and wrap her arms around the pipe.

"Merciful heavens!" She'd come close to being the only apprentice cupid in celestial history to get herself killed by falling off a roof. Assuming cupids could die. And she didn't want to be the first to test that possibility.

"Are you all right?"

"Yes." Her voice cracked.

The tin vent pipe bent, threatening to break loose. She screamed. Her feet scrambled against the slippery shingles.

"Hang on. I'm coming down to get you."

She heard a thump, and her stomach changed places with her heart. Then the flashlight came hurtling past her, spinning around and around as it flew off the roof.

That's when she felt the first drops of rain. The deluge came an instant later. Scrunching her eyes closed, she sent up a heartfelt prayer.

BLAKE HAD NEVER BEEN so scared in his entire life.

He didn't know how he managed to get her back up to the widow's walk, but when they reached it Eloise was shaking uncontrollably. He was cold, too, and they were both drenched to the skin.

"I'll get you downstairs so you can get out of those wet clothes," he told her. "You'll be warmed up in no time." He opened the door to the small rooftop sanctuary and stepped inside. The absence of rain and wind pounding in his face was a relief.

"I was afraid...the door might have...l-locked,"

she said, shivering, her teeth chattering, "w-when it blew closed."

"No problem." He bent to lift the trapdoor. Frowning, he gave it a tug. How the hell could it have blown shut? The outside door, he understood. But not this.

He gave it another yank. Nothing.

Kneeling, he pounded on the floor. "Anybody down there? Can you hear us?"

"What's w-wrong?"

"The door's stuck. I can't seem to get it open."

She groaned a soft, whimpering, shivery sound.

Damn it! He had to get her warm. Frantically, he looked around the room, his gaze landing on the narrow cot beneath the east wall. A blanket!

"Take off your clothes, angel. We'll both catch our death if we don't get warm soon." It wasn't so much that the temperature was particularly cold, but that the soaking had chilled them both bone-deep. No way was Blake going to be responsible for Eloise catching pneumonia.

"I can't, Blake. I've never been nude—"

"Do it, angel, or I'll do it for you." He stripped off his own shirt, shucked his shoes and shed his pants. She turned her back and began to remove her clothes. He threw back the spread from the cot, found a second, cleaner blanket, and gave it a shake before he wrapped it around her. It wasn't that he was so darn noble he wasn't tempted to sneak a peek. In this case, he was far more concerned about avoiding hypothermia. For both of them.

"Sit down, honey. Wrap up good."

He eased her down onto the cot. She pulled up her legs, tucking them under her. Draping the tatty bedspread around himself, he sat beside her and pulled her into his arms. They'd share whatever heat they could.

"I was so afraid I was going to lose you," he whispered, his lips pressed to her temple. The truth of that realization shook him more than the goose bumps that covered his body. "God help me, I don't know what I'd do if that happened. I love you, Eloise."

She went very still. Even her shivers stopped. "You don't mean that, Blake," she said, her voice firm and insistent.

"I know we've only just met and it sounds a little crazy—"

"No. What you're feeling is...well, a mistake."

His brows lowered. A fear so deep it wrenched through his gut shook him. "My God, Eloise, are you married? Is there someone else?"

"That's not the problem. It's..." She turned and looked up into his eyes. "I'm an apprentice cupid. I was sent here to...well, get you to fall in love, all right. But when I shot my arrow, I...missed." Her lips twisted into a forced smile and her gaze lowered. "I shot myself in the foot."

Oh, sure, that made a lot of sense. And worried the hell out of Blake. Not only had Eloise been chilled to the bone by her ordeal on the roof, some weird part of her brain had been frozen, too.

"It's okay, angel. I'm not going to rush you into—"

"But it's true. See, I was transferred to Cupid's Celestial Division after I messed up my assignments as a guardian angel."

He blinked. "You're my guardian angel?"

"No, not yours. On my last case I was assigned to help this really nice young woman who thought nobody loved her and she was super depressed so she was going to jump off this big bridge that they'd just built over a river in this little town in Oregon."

"So you stopped her." As if that thought made any sense.

"Not exactly. I was getting ready to, you understand, when I noticed this really sweet little old lady walking along with her grocery cart. She was just about to step out in front of this humongous truck and I couldn't let that happen."

"No, of course not." He'd had no idea Eloise had such a vivid imagination.

"So I raced over and pulled her back onto the sidewalk."

"That's great. Really great."

"I knew you'd understand. But that left me with this other problem. The woman who I was supposed to be guarding had already jumped into the river."

Blake's head was spinning. She seemed so sincere... "So what did you do?"

"Well, since they were having the ceremony to open this new bridge, with a ribbon cutting and all, I pushed the mayor into the river."

Blake coughed and sputtered. "Why the hell did you do that?"

"Because the mayor had been an Olympic swimmer. I'd seen that in his file and had been really impressed. So he pulled the young lady out in no time at all. That made him a hero, and I understand he's been elected to two more terms." She shrugged. "But my boss wasn't exactly pleased with how I had handled the situation."

"So that's how you became a cupid?" They'd both stopped shivering, so Blake slid across the cot to rest his back against the wall and he brought Eloise with him. The rain was still tattooing the roof with an incessant beat. He didn't mind as long as she was in his arms.

"They might have transferred me somewhere else, but I had already blown my assignment in the Baby Department."

"Babies? You like babies?" He could relate to that, he thought as he slid his hand across her midsection. He'd love to plant the seed that would make her belly fill with *his* baby.

"Oh, yes. I loved working with the babies. But I sort of overstepped my bounds."

Why was he not surprised? "You want to tell me about it?"

"I thought I was doing the right thing."

"I'm listening." She turned toward him, and he brushed a soft kiss across her forehead. Even half-drenched, she smelled and tasted heavenly.

"There was this little boy. He was absolutely adorable. But no one had picked him. I don't know why. He just didn't seem to fit, you know? And then I thought... Well, there was this wonderful, loving couple that was about to have a baby, one I'd picked out for them that was such a perfect match. But they'd tried really hard for years to get the woman pregnant and I thought..." She took a deep breath that raised the blanket over her full breasts. "Kind of at the last minute I sent the other little boy along as his twin."

"You're joking," he sputtered.

"They were surprised—and so was their doctor— but I don't think anybody was all that unhappy. Except my boss, of course."

"Of course."

"He didn't understand how awful it is to go years and years and years without anybody picking you, especially when you're a baby." Her eyes brimmed with tears. "I did."

"You weren't ever picked." However wild and fanciful her story might be, it didn't take a genius to know Eloise felt as though no one would want her. She was wrong. Blake wanted her more than life itself.

With a dejected shake of her head, she whispered, "Never."

"And that's why you became a cupid." He understood it as a metaphor for her eternal pursuit of love.

"Actually it had to do with a new affirmative action program they'd started. I'm the first woman in the department." She lifted her chin slightly. "It's very important that I succeed. For women, I mean."

"Affirmative action programs are old hat, Eloise. A lot of places are doing away with them and you're telling me—"

"They're very slow about initiating innovative ideas where I come from, particularly those that are politically sensitive. Pretty conservative, you know? I don't want to ruin the chances other women might have."

"So you became a cupid."

"I'd already failed remedial harp lessons." She hiccuped and her chin quivered. "Twice."

"You know, harp music is okay, I suppose. But the sweetest music in the world is a man and woman singing an even older tune."

A born skeptic who'd grown up in the school of hard knocks, he couldn't possibly believe her story about being a cupid, or a guardian angel. It didn't matter. He felt something with this woman he'd never felt before. As far as he was concerned, she could make up as many wild stories as she liked—invent whole novels, if that's what it took to make her happy.

Holding her face gently between his hands, he kissed her. From this moment on, he'd show her how much she was wanted. By him.

8

IT WAS THE MOST NATURAL thing on earth for Eloise to go into Blake's arms, to accept his kiss and return it with a matching fervor. She'd told him that she was an apprentice cupid, confident there wasn't a chance in heaven or hell he'd believe her. Her story would destroy his trust. Hubert had promised that would also destroy his love.

But like the failed antidote, nothing seemed to change Blake's mind. No longer would she fight the forces that were beyond her control. For tonight, she would enjoy the taste of forbidden fruit, even though tomorrow she'd have to face the consequences of her foolish heart.

"Heaven help me, angel. You are so beautiful, so deliciously desirable." His words were a prayer on her lips, a balm to her femininity, a hymn to her heart. "I'm never going to stop wanting you."

He tasted of sweet sugared coffee and smelled as fresh as the rain that had drenched them. The damp strands of his hair clung to her fingers as she held him.

The blanket slid from her shoulder. His mouth claimed her breast while his long, tapered fingers held her close. He suckled her, tugging gently, and her body clenched as though he were kissing her in a far more intimate place.

She moaned at the keen pleasure that shot through her.

"Blake, I..."

"I know, love. I know."

In the distance, thunder rumbled. Another flash of lightning spotlighted them as though it were full daylight—Blake's head at her breast, her arms holding him close. In this small room they were on top of the world, at the center where storms swirled and built in intensity before bursting from the press of unrelenting power.

Eloise felt it, ached with it, arched her back to him with the need for more. She'd never been so aware of her earthly surroundings—the coarse fabric of the blanket along her shoulder blades, the roughness of his evening whiskers on her flesh wherever he kissed her, the tart, masculine scent of him, his unique flavor as she ran her tongue over him. The rain-soaked air chilled her; his hands warmed her, inside and out. Tenderly.

She couldn't breathe. The blood pounded through her veins. She sobbed his name, a prayer and a chant.

In the next flash of lightning, she saw him above her, his expression intent, his features caught in a beautiful tabloid of masculinity. His eyes were dark, his firm jaw clenched. He was a dark-haired Adonis, a gladiator, a champion of men.

And then she felt him between her legs, pleading

for entry. She granted him his wish. Joyously. Without remorse. Eager as he, she relished the sensation of him filling her, stretching her beyond what she had imagined possible.

"You're so tight, angel. I don't want to hurt you."

"You won't. Unless you stop."

Lifting her hips, she finished what he had started, ignoring the slight discomfort she felt in exchange for knowing the full pleasure of being a woman. She lay still for a moment, adjusting to his size, the miracle of how they fit together with such perfection. And then he began to move inside her.

"Oh, my..." Her voice caught, her mind faltered.

She'd never realized the heat of such intimate friction could turn her insides to hot, flowing lava. She burned with it, with him. It pooled in her, raced through her. Without thought, she offered up her body to it. And then she burst from the awesome power in an anthem of jubilation.

"Bla...ake!"

"Yes." He plunged into her again, spinning her through a universe she'd never before seen or knew existed, and soon he followed.

Sometime later she lay in his arms, still connected, a part of him, and he a part of her. Her body still pulsed with passion, with sensations so beautiful, tears slid from the corners of her eyes.

"Don't cry, sweetheart. Please don't cry." Reverently, he kissed the tears from her cheeks. "I didn't mean to hurt you."

She shook her head. "You didn't." But now she'd

gained an inkling of what Margaret had meant about a man being good in bed. Blake must surely be exceptional; she'd never dreamed there could be such a potent connection between two people. Eloise thought she'd keep that amazing revelation to herself.

"I wanted you so much," he whispered.

"It's the magic potion. Cupid's dart."

"It's *you,* Eloise. Only you." He lifted his weight from her and rolled onto his side, bringing her with him, holding her close. Gently, he pulled the blanket around her shoulders.

Eloise thought her heart might truly break. He hadn't believed her. He'd listened, but he hadn't understood.

Resting her head on his shoulder, she listened to his steady breathing, felt his heart beat, all the time wondering what on earth she should do next. She'd probably violated every rule in the heavenly book by making love with Blake and put celestial affirmative action at risk in the process, not to mention the damage she'd done to her own career. Once again she had failed. Dismally.

To her own dismay, she wasn't in the least contrite. Not about her future, at any rate.

She'd willingly spend the rest of eternity sweeping up bits of flyaway clouds and cleaning dusty angel wings in exchange for these few earthly minutes she'd spent in Blake's arms.

But somehow she had to make up for her slip in behavior to Blake—not Hubert. It was Blake who would be left behind when she returned to her celestial home. He deserved the promotion he'd worked so hard to achieve; he had earned his happiness here on earth. They hadn't found the clue they'd been searching for on the roof. Tomorrow she'd redouble her efforts to help him.

But right now she'd indulge herself a little longer in the comfort and warmth of his arms. The memory, she knew, would have to last her a very long time.

"THAT'S DAMNED ODD." Squatting, Blake hefted the trapdoor of the lookout room as easily as if it were spring balanced.

"What's wrong?" Eloise asked. She was just hooking her skirt around her waist, her hair still a mussed tangle of blond curls from their night together. The faint glow of shy awareness colored her cheeks. In the dawn light, she looked as beautiful as any woman he'd ever known.

"I thought we'd be out there on the roof for half the day trying to attract somebody's attention to rescue us. This door opened so easily, I can't believe it was ever stuck."

"Maybe the rain got into the mechanism somehow."

"Could be, I suppose." But Blake didn't think so. It was more like someone had *locked* them in the lookout room, just like they'd been trapped in the ballroom. But why? And who? Margaret seemed the obvious choice. She was devious enough. But it sure as hell didn't make a lot of sense.

Not that Blake minded having spent the night with

Eloise. Whoever had apparently thrown the bolt on the underside of the door had done him a huge favor.

Instantly Blake's body reacted to the memory of Eloise in his arms, her passionate response to his lovemaking as eager and hungry as his own. Every part of her body tasted of heaven. Soft and pliable, she had molded to him like warm velvet. The night had been endless—yet over much too soon.

Checking his watch, he realized he'd totally lost track of the time during the night, lost track of his obligations. If he didn't suspect she was a little tender after the number of times they had made love during the darkness, he'd take her again now and forget about Crankshank.

But he couldn't forget about Stevie.

He extended his hand to Eloise. "You ready to face the world?"

She took a shuddering breath. "Barely." Her fingers trembled as she clasped his hand.

"Regrets?"

Her blue eyes locked with his and she swallowed visibly. "None worth mentioning."

"I want you to know, being with you last night was as special to me as anything that's ever happened in my life." She'd been so tight, he'd wondered if she'd been a virgin. But she hadn't objected. He doubted if he could have stopped himself if she had. With her free spirit, her eager response, it hardly seemed possible that he'd been her first lover. And he refused to dwell on the thought that some other man had held her and loved her before him.

He also refused to give any credence to her cock-amamie tale about being an apprentice cupid. He'd chalk that one up to a vivid imagination and a lifetime of loneliness.

"It was special for me, too." She smiled tremulously. "We'd better go. You still have clues to find."

"Yeah."

He preceded her down the ladder, holding her elbow to steady her as she reached the third-floor hallway.

"I'm going to change," he said, looking at his rumpled shirt and trousers. "Looks like I slept in these."

Her lips curled into a cute little grin. "But I know better, don't I?"

Damned if he didn't blush.

He was still blushing as Terry came out of his room. He gave them a quick perusal that took in their mussed appearance, then glanced toward the open trapdoor above the stairs. "You two been up on the roof?"

"Looking for clues," Blake said, covering their discovery as best he could. "Something about shingles."

"Find anything?"

Blake had found the woman he wanted to spend the rest of his life with, but he wasn't about to admit that to Terry. "Uh, not this time. You know how obtuse Crankshank's clues can be. Nothing is as easy as it seems."

Terry shrugged. "I saw a pile of old shingles out

by the storage shed in back. Maybe what you're looking for is there.''

"Hey, thanks a lot. We'll give it a try."

"No problem," Terry said. "As soon as I've finished breakfast, I'm back to the trenches. We figure to find that ol' pirate treasure by noon. Then Crankshank is going to be missing a whole lot of regional sales directors."

"For your sake, I hope you're right," Blake said, meaning it. Because if Crankshank ever learned how disloyal his staff was there'd be a lot of termination notices issued.

As Terry wandered off down the hallway, Blake glanced at Eloise. The corners of her lips quivered in an effort to suppress a smile, her eyes crinkled, and a little giggle escaped.

"What?" he asked, frowning.

"We nearly broke our necks last night, Blake. If we'd waited till morning and looked outside—"

"We wouldn't have had nearly so much fun," he told her.

Her smile softened and a dreamy look came into her eyes. "You're right." She reached up and kissed him softly. "Did I remember to say thank you? I've never experienced anything so wonderful."

"My pleasure, ma'am. The feeling is definitely mutual."

They walked down the hall together. As they reached her door, she glanced back over her shoulder the way they had come. "Doesn't it seem to you there ought to be another door along here?"

He followed the direction of her gaze. He'd been to these retreats a half dozen times. He didn't see anything wrong. "Why do you ask that?"

"Terry came out of that room right next to the roof access. But if his room is next to mine, then it's got to be huge."

"I see what you mean." There was a long expanse of wall between Eloise's door and Terry's, broken only by a slight variation in the shade of the washed-out wallpaper. "Maybe they gave him a suite. He probably arrived first to brownnose with Crankshank and claimed the best room in the house before anybody else showed up."

"Hmm." She nodded thoughtfully. "You're probably right." But she'd spent a lot of time between heavenly assignments doing jigsaw puzzles. Something about these pieces didn't seem to fit.

WHEN THEY'D CHANGED clothes, they went down to breakfast, though Eloise could eat little. After tasting paradise with Blake—and knowing she'd soon lose him—her appetite had vanished. Flavors she'd always cherished on her visits to earth now seemed bland; her throat felt constricted by the future she didn't want to face.

They went outside in search of the storage shed Terry had mentioned and the shingles where Blake's clue might be hidden. The sky had cleared following the storm, and a mockingbird called from a high cypress branch that moved lazily in the breeze.

"If we find this clue, how many more will there be?" she asked.

"We're getting close to the end. The grand finale is tonight at a costume banquet."

She shot him a look. "Costume?"

"Don't worry about it. Appearing in costume is one of Crankshank's quirks. He likes to play at being a pirate, in honor of his ancestors. He provides the outfits he wants us to wear."

Or in Eloise's case, Hubert did. She could just imagine what ridiculous costume he had chosen for her.

The door to the shed creaked open, the hinges rusted from disuse. Only dim light filtered inside.

"I'm sorry I lost that damn flashlight off the roof," Blake mumbled.

"You could go find another one."

"No, this is fine."

He began rummaging around inside, at one point grunting sharply as though he'd banged his shin. Then he reappeared at the doorway. "I'll be damned if I can find anything in there. Maybe we ought to take up with Terry after all and look for the pirate treasure."

"You could take your penalty points. Only you, Spencer and Bob are still in the game. Plus Margaret, of course."

"You've got that damn straight." He shoved a fallen lock of dark hair back from his forehead. "I don't care so much about Spencer, but I damn well don't want Margaret to beat me."

"She's the woman you were supposed to fall in love with."

He sent her a quelling look. "Not in this lifetime."

"It would help my job prospects if you did." And those of other celestial females, too. Not that they didn't usually enjoy their current assignments, Eloise was sure, but no opportunities should be shut to them.

And what of Blake's unborn baby? What would become of him if Blake and Margaret never got together? Eloise shuddered at the thought of a dark-eyed child waiting endlessly to be chosen.

Looping an arm around her shoulders, Blake headed them back toward the house, ignoring her continued references to her matchmaking assignment. They hadn't gone far when Blake halted abruptly.

"I hate it when he does that," he said.

"Who does what?"

"Crankshank." Blake pointed to a single shingle propped against a post beside the walkway. "He put the damn thing right in front of our noses. Like the clue said, it's a wonder we didn't fall over it."

Kneeling, Blake picked up the shingle and flipped it over. A note was attached to the underside.

"*The one with balls is inside these walls,*'" he read aloud and groaned.

"What walls?" she asked, growing as weary as Blake of Crankshank's game. "And what balls?"

He shook his head. "If I had to guess, I'd say there was a pool table somewhere in the house. Or a Ping-Pong table. For all I know, there could be a basketball court in the basement." He stood back and gazed up at the top of the mansion. "Hell, it could be the world globe in the parlor room. That's a ball of sorts. At this point, I simply don't know."

She hooked her hand through his arm. "Don't get discouraged. We've found all the other clues. We'll find this one, too."

In a quick gesture, he touched his lips to her forehead. "Frankly, I'm tempted to call it a day, take you back up to my room, and continue where we left off last night."

A pleasurable flush warmed her cheeks. She'd enjoy that, too. But his future was her priority and that meant they had to struggle on in search of the next clue.

From the south end of the island, Eloise heard a ruckus, men yelling and shouting. Ettienne appeared at a dead run, a pickax swinging dangerously in his hand.

"What's going on?" Blake shouted.

"We've reached the foundation of the house. We're going to have to blast our way through."

Eloise shot an anxious look at Blake. "Blast?" Good heavens! With her propensity for slight errors in judgment, she'd never argued with her superiors that she didn't belong anywhere near TNT. And this was a very small island.

"Those guys have lost it." Blake sighed. "Maybe with Spencer's help I can stop them from bringing the whole damn house down. Crankshank's always been a little screwy about his treasure hunt, but this time I think he's gone too far."

THE WHOLE HOUSE SHUDDERED as pickaxes and who-knew-what-else slammed into the foundation. So far there hadn't been any explosions.

"I think we need to stop them," Blake said. He'd found Spencer and Bob in the dining room, the only ones who'd appeared in time for lunch. Eloise had run upstairs to freshen up but hadn't yet returned. "Thank God the pneumatic drill and dynamite they've ordered from the mainland haven't come yet."

"I quite agree." As Spencer nodded, the rolls of fat that made up his double chin compressed. "Outside of physically standing in their way—which, given their enthusiasm, doesn't seem to be a wise idea—I'm not sure how we can stop them from taking this house apart brick by brick."

"This house has been standing for more than a hundred years," Blake said. "I'd hate to see it collapse under the weight of their stupidity." And Crankshank's quirky management style, he mentally added.

Bob piped up. "I'll go down in the basement if you want me to."

"That's all right, son," Spencer said, with only the slightest trace of indulgence. "My guess is Obadiah's hoping to enlarge his basement, anyway. Why don't you check in the kitchen to see how they're doing with our lunch?"

Eager to do his mentor's bidding, Bob hurried from the room.

Blake slid his hands into his pockets. "That youngster reminds me of myself ten years ago—so damn eager.'' A kid from the roughest neighborhood in town, Blake had clawed his way up the ladder. Honestly. Bringing his family to a safer place with him. But sometimes the raw edges were still sharp, his instinct to use fists instead of reason still apparent. Spencer, and Crankshank, had both helped him through the transition. He respected them both.

''You've got that straight.'' Chuckling softly, Spencer lowered himself into the chair at the head of the table. ''You haven't forgotten what your goals are, I trust?''

''Not a chance.'' Though some of his goals had taken a back seat since he'd met Eloise and made love with her. In or out of sight, she was constantly on his mind. No matter what happened here on the island, he was sure that would continue. He simply wasn't sure what he could offer her. With all of his obligations, she'd be the last person he'd want to shortchange and he was afraid that's exactly what would happen. He wouldn't want Eloise to suffer the same bitter disappointment his sister and mother had experienced when they'd counted on love—not to mention the way Stevie was suffering indirectly.

A crashing sound occurred somewhere above them. Wood splintered, glass shattered and a heavy object hit the floor.

''What the hell was that?'' Blake asked, wincing. He looked up, half expecting the plaster ceiling to collapse on them. He rose to investigate but Spencer motioned for him to stay put.

"It's Margaret. She thinks the answer to her next clue is somewhere in the house. I imagine she'll let us know if she needs any help."

"She's one hell of a determined lady," Blake conceded. Perhaps winning the promotion was just as important to Margaret as it was to Blake.

"You and Eloise seem to be getting along just fine," Spencer said.

Unwilling to comment about his relationship with Eloise, Blake simply nodded.

"Which region did she say she was from?" Spencer asked.

"I'm not, uh, exactly sure." From the farthest one, she'd said. But she'd also told him a wild story about her being an apprentice cupid, which he didn't believe for a moment. On the other hand, where else could she have come from? "You know of any new regions that have opened lately?"

"Haven't heard a word." From the relish tray sitting on the table, Spencer selected a celery stick. He dipped it into a bowl of blue cheese dressing.

The house shook one more time.

"If we don't do something soon," Blake said, "we're going to find ourselves surrounded by nothing more than a pile of toothpicks."

"You're right." Spencer levered himself to his feet. "I like her, by the way."

"Who?" Surely he couldn't mean Margaret.

His wrinkles and folds of fat stretched into a smile that made him look much younger. "Eloise. Who else? You could do a lot worse, Blake. If I could, I'd give you a bit of competition but I think she's already hooked on you. In which case, I wish you luck. With her at your side, there'd be no limit to your future.''

Blake was stunned by Spencer's evaluation. As crazy as it was, after only three days, he had no doubt about his feelings for Eloise. But how could Spencer—who didn't always seem to be the most perceptive guy—have caught on to the depth of those feelings? Especially since they were emotions he still wasn't entirely willing to admit to anyone else and wasn't quite sure what to do about.

''You're looking pretty serious there, Blake.'' Spencer slapped him on the back. ''I want you to know if you've got a problem—any kind of a problem except woman troubles, that is—I'll do anything I can to help.''

''Thanks, Spencer. But I'll be okay.'' It was never easy for Blake to admit he had a problem, much less needed help.

Shrugging, Spencer headed into the kitchen, which provided access to the basement. Blake went upstairs, lured by the frantic pounding that came from the second floor.

He found Margaret on her knees prying walnut wainscotting away from the wall in the hallway.

''What are you doing?''

''My clue.'' She looked up at him, wild-eyed. Her cheeks were flushed, her breathing accelerated. ''It's here somewhere. This is the last one. I know it is. If I can just find it—''

''Balls?''

"In these damn walls! They're here somewhere."

"That's the same clue I've got. It must be the final one."

"And I'm going to find it." She ripped a board loose. There was nothing but plaster behind it.

"You're pressing too hard, Margaret. It's not worth it."

"Easy for you to say." Frantically, she glanced up and down the hallway. "My parents expect me to be so damn perfect. They've been on my case for years that I'm *only* a regional director. If they only knew…" Tears glistened in her eyes.

"I'm sorry, Margaret. I didn't realize." He'd never seen anyone so manic, so close to going over the edge. Sympathetically, he placed his hand on her shoulder.

She lurched away from him, her face going chalky white. "Don't."

"I'm not going to hurt you. I just think you ought to come downstairs. Lunch is ready—"

"I haven't solved my damn clue yet."

"I haven't solved it, either. That means we're even."

"What about Spencer?"

"He didn't say. But he missed a couple of clues yesterday. I don't think you have anything to worry about." Blake wondered if he had ever approached Crankshank's treasure hunt with the same intensity Margaret was demonstrating. Probably so. This year included, given the high stakes resting on the outcome.

Using the wall to steady herself as she stood, Margaret said, "I'll keep looking for a few more minutes. Then I'll throw in the towel until after lunch."

Blake shrugged. "Your choice. Try not to tear down the whole house. We need something to come back to next year."

When he went downstairs he discovered Eloise had returned. Her welcoming smile tightened a spot in his chest, warming him.

He leaned his shoulder against the door into the dining room, content to leisurely admire the way her white dress pulled tight over her breasts and rested softly over the swell of her hips. "If you're a cupid, how did you get down to earth?"

"I rode a sunbeam," she said, not missing a beat.

"A reasonable explanation. Does that mean you can't appear after dark?"

"Oh, no. At night we travel on moonbeams. But that's a little more dangerous since we can't see where we're going. And my aim isn't too accurate anyway."

God, he loved her imagination! Though her story certainly explained why she'd slammed into him on the ferry.

The front door flew open and Terry burst in, shovel in hand. He raced down the hallway toward the kitchen. "We're almost there. We think there's a secret room in the basement. Ettienne is breaking through from the outside and I'm going to try..." His voice faded as he sprinted out of sight.

"The secret room isn't downstairs," Eloise said

softly. "At least if one is there, it's not the only one in the house."

Blake's head snapped around. "What do you mean?"

"While I was upstairs just now, I heard someone moving around in the room next to mine."

"Maybe Terry was up there—"

"He was outside, Blake, in his precious tunnel. I can account for everyone's whereabouts who's supposed to be on the island, but I still heard someone in the room next to mine. And yesterday I saw movement at the curtains in that room."

Blake's forehead furrowed. *The one with balls is inside these walls.* Smiling, he said, "I think I know who's upstairs. I should have suspected a trick from the beginning, and then when you asked me about who drank strawberry tea—"

Hubert huffed downstairs in a hurried clip. "I have orders from Mr. C to stop all this nonsense."

"I knew it!" Blake said.

Simultaneously, Eloise asked, "He's here?"

Hubert eyed her disparagingly. "My dear, he has been here the entire time."

High heels clicking as she ran down the stairs, Margaret appeared. "I've found him!" she cried, breathlessly. "I win! I win! Game's over!"

Blake muttered a curse. Damn! He'd come so close.

9

HER COSTUME, the gown of a Roman goddess, was actually quite effective. Eloise supposed she should be grateful for that. The new supply of Cupid's magic darts that Hubert had provided should have pleased her, too.

Her hand trembled as she held them gingerly in her palm.

She'd been given a second chance. This time when she took aim and let the darts fly, Blake would fall in love with Margaret. And she with him.

An ache filled Eloise's chest and her throat constricted. Could she actually bring herself to do the deed when the opportunity arrived? The thought of Blake loving another woman was so painful, so contrary to what her instincts cried out for, she could barely breathe, let alone see through the blur of her tears.

And yet, what else could she do?

She'd been sent to earth for this very purpose. To refuse to carry out her assignment now was tantamount to rebellion. That simply didn't happen where she came from. Or if it did—as Lucifer had discovered—the results were banishment.

Tomorrow, no matter what else happened, she would have to return to her home and face the music. She suspected failure meant the music would be anything but heavenly.

And failure also meant that those women who might want to follow in her none-too-steady footsteps would never have the chance. She owed them more than that. Love, after all, was a subject that women knew best.

Sighing tremulously, she closed her fingers over the darts and slid them into the golden quiver pinned to her dress. She didn't drop a single one. Though she wanted to. Desperately.

Earlier, when Blake had knocked on their connecting door inviting her to go downstairs with him for pre-dinner cocktails, she'd begged off. "Not quite ready," she'd told him. And in her heart, she still wasn't ready for what she'd have to do.

She lifted her chin. The time had come. She could delay no longer.

The hallway was empty. Walking slowly, she reached the stairs and descended. Gone were the days when she'd be tempted to slide down the banister. She doubted she'd ever feel that carefree and happy again. Dear heaven! Is that what a broken heart did to a human?

The others were just dispersing after their pre-dinner drinks. Hubert bustled about, shooing them from the parlor into the dining room.

"I trust you found the darts," he said under his breath.

"Yes."

"And you know what to do with them?"

"I know." The words scraped her throat as though they were razor blades.

He picked up a dirty glass from a small table and placed it on his tray. Before he could walk away, she snared him by the arm.

"You told me there weren't any more darts available," she said, her tone accusing him of the lie he'd obviously told her. "What made you change your mind?"

He looked down his button nose at her hand on his arm. "If you must know, I received orders from upstairs to make a new supply available to you."

"From Crankshank? Why on earth would he—"

"My dear, I take my orders from a much higher authority than Mr. Crankshank."

"Yes, of course." How could she have forgotten?

"Now, if you will unhand me...I have work to do. And so do you."

She stood uncertainly for a moment watching Hubert waddle away on his short-legged gait.

"You're the most beautiful Venus I've ever seen," Blake whispered, coming up behind her to place a kiss at her nape. "My goddess of love."

A pleasurable shiver sped down her spine. She turned and smiled. Her eyes widened in surprise. "And you make a perfect knight in shining armor, Sir Blake."

"I clank when I walk," he said with a wry smile as he offered her his arm. "Shall we dine, m'lady?"

By the time they entered the dining room, the others had taken their seats. Ettienne appeared foolish in his court jester's costume; Bob was no less uncomfortable in his Blue Boy frills, velvet suit and tights. On the opposite side of the table, Terry was at ease in his Don Juan attire, although Margaret as Elvira did not appear receptive to his advances. Spencer looked like a combination Samurai warrior and sumo wrestler.

At the head of the table was Crankshank himself in Black Beard regalia, an impressive figure of a man even with an eye patch and thinning gray hair. With a slight smile of acknowledgment, he nodded to Eloise.

"Ah, at last we are all together," he said, raising his wineglass. "A toast to another successful corporate retreat. A most enlightening and entertaining experience."

Reluctantly, Blake drank from his glass. The entire ordeal might have been entertaining for Crankshank but the key players hadn't all enjoyed it. Particularly when they'd learned Obadiah had been spying on them from the beginning, lurking in that hidden room upstairs, as Eloise has suspected. Blake felt used. He imagined the others did, too.

"If Hubert will be so kind as to serve us," Crankshank said, "I will inform you just how much I have learned from this year's exercise. And how much each of you *failed* to learn from prior years."

Most of the diners at the table focused their attention on their silverware, finding something fascinating about the swirled pattern.

"It was perhaps not a wise choice of mine to seed the island with that doubloon," Crankshank conceded.

"You put it there?" Ettienne asked, his head coming up with a jingle as the bell on his cap bobbed.

"I did, indeed. I intended it to be a distraction from the true goal of the treasure hunt. I had no idea half of you would pursue a fictional treasure to the exclusion of your original purpose."

Terry said, "If we'd found the pirate's buried treasure—"

"Impossible. There's never been any such thing. The entire story of one of my ancestors being a pirate is hogwash. He was a blockade runner, a noble profession in our country's history."

"But you must have known when you planted the doubloon that we'd—"

"Try to tear down my house? I had not expected you to order dynamite."

"Then what was the point?" Blake asked.

"To see how all of you would react, of course."

At least he and Eloise hadn't been distracted by the gold piece, Blake thought. That gave him some hope the promotion would still be his. If that happened...

"As it turned out," Crankshank continued, leaning back in his chair while Hubert removed his soup dish and delivered a lobster dinner in its place, "my counterfeit doubloon—"

"Counterfeit?" Ettienne coughed and sputtered, spraying a spoonful of soup halfway across the table.

Bob patted his back.

Crankshank arched his brows. With a quick flick of his hand, he snapped his black eye patch off and tossed it aside. "Apparently you have no idea how much an original doubloon would be worth. Only a fool would risk losing an authentic coin like that."

Ettienne slunk down in his chair. Blake felt sorry for him. His Louisiana region had been doing well under his leadership but this trip to Georgia might well have dealt him a death knell in terms of his career with Crest Enterprises.

"Not all of us fell for your diversion, Obadiah," Margaret reminded him, oh, so sweetly.

"That's true," he agreed. Expertly he cracked his lobster. "You were certainly committed to searching out the clues. Narrow-mindedly so."

"I pride myself on my ability to focus solely on my work," she said, a proud lift to her chin. "My parents always made it a point to—"

"Admirable, of course. But not necessarily ideal for someone whose concerns must reach beyond his or her own self-interest. Managers are best when they think of others first."

Margaret paled. "But that's what I thought you wanted—a winner who'd found all the clues."

From where Blake was sitting, he wondered if she was about to throw up. He wouldn't have blamed her. In spite of discovering all of the clues, including

Crankshank's whereabouts, it was clear the big promotion wouldn't be hers.

Blake sat up a little straighter as Crankshank's gaze cruised down to his end of the table.

"I believe Ms. Periwinkle has been the most pleasant surprise of this year's retreat," he said, focusing on Eloise instead of Blake.

"I'm not eligible for the promotion," she said hastily.

His lips curled into the smile of a sly old fox. "I'm quite aware of that, but you have provided this old man with more joy than he has experienced in a good many years."

Her cheeks colored.

In spite of Crankshank's age, Blake's testosterone surged and his possessive instincts went on high alert. He extended his arm across the back of her chair. *She's mine,* he mentally transmitted, the tin shoulder hinge on his costume squeaking.

Obadiah ignored the message. "If it were possible, I'd promote you to a rank I esteem more than any other."

Margaret said, "You can't bring in someone new. Not at this point—"

Crankshank silenced her by raising his hand. "I was referring to the rank of *wife*. To my great delight, for the past forty-some years that position has been filled. I'd doubt she'd welcome an interloper any more than you would, however charming the young lady." He dipped his head regally to Eloise, then turned his gaze toward Blake. "The fact that you and

Ms. Periwinkle worked so well together was a plus for you, Blake. I was particularly eager to observe your, uh, teamwork."

Unwilling to be outpraised, Terry said, "Under my leadership, our team worked together like clockwork."

Crankshank sent him a quelling look. "For the *wrong* goal."

Terry's bravado faded like the eagerness of a salesman who'd had the door slammed in his face.

Turning to Spencer, Crankshank smiled. "You failed to discover many of the clues, Spencer. The penalty points added up."

"My fault, I'm afraid." With a self-deprecating gesture, he indicated his treasure-hunting partner. "Bob certainly gave it a good try, though. Worked as hard as anyone could ask. I think if we'd had more time—"

"And more people on your team," Crankshank noted. "It seems to me you were willing to work with anyone who'd join you."

"Of course, sir. I know my limitations. And the more people working toward the same goal, the more likely it is you'll succeed."

"Precisely." Crankshank leaned back in his chair and tented his fingers in front of his mouth, thoughtfully glancing around the room at his sales directors.

Blake got a sick feeling in the pit of his stomach. Spencer was going to get the promotion. And the bonus. Blake had failed. And the worst part was, he couldn't fault Crankshank's decision. Of all the regional managers, Spencer had demonstrated he was the best company man. It was right that that should count for something.

Somehow Blake would have to find another way to pay Stevie's medical bills, even if it meant going into debt himself.

Around the table, Crankshank's unspoken message began to sink in.

"Hey, Spencer," Bob spoke up. "Congratulations. I'm looking forward to working for you."

"Yeah. Right," Terry mumbled under his breath.

Others joined in a chorus of halfhearted congratulations. Crankshank did nothing to suggest they'd gotten the wrong idea. Spencer was his man.

Under the table, and out of sight of anyone else, Eloise placed her hand on Blake's thigh. "I'm sorry," she whispered, devastated that he hadn't won the promotion he so coveted. "I'm sorry. It's my fault. If I hadn't—"

"Don't be ridiculous. Spencer won the contest fair and square. We just didn't know the rules."

If he had known what was expected of him, Eloise was sure Blake would have moved heaven and earth to earn that promotion himself. And she'd done nothing to help him. As usual, all her efforts had led to failure. Perhaps if he'd teamed up with Margaret—someone experienced with business and familiar with Crankshank's wily ways—they would have figured out what the old man was up to together.

Eloise gazed across the table at the woman in question—her target. Margaret's black wig had slipped slightly askew. Her cleavage was shown to full advantage in a gaping vee of black lace, providing a perfect bull's-eye right next to her heart.

Swallowing hard, Eloise decided the moment had come. Blake hadn't won the promotion. A woman to love—a lifetime companion—would be his consolation prize. He deserved that much and more.

Surreptitiously, she plucked the miniature bow from the pin on her chest and selected an arrow from the quiver. She handled it carefully, the invisible shaft almost slipping between her fingertips before she could gain a good grip. Regret tightened her throat. If only she hadn't learned about the power of love, this assignment would be so much easier.

She lifted the bow and arrow. Her hands shook. Tears burned at the backs of her eyes and she blinked them away. She let the magic dart fly.

Margaret's hand flew to her chest. With one cough, she brushed the offending missile away, then straightened in her chair, looking around the table as if to spot the source of the stinging dart.

Before Eloise took time to think, she extracted another dart from her quiver and jammed it muscle-deep into Blake's thigh.

"Ouch! What the hell?" He caught her wrist. "What are you doing?"

Breaking my own heart. "Look," she told him. "Margaret has a glint in her eye."

As ordered, he glanced across the table. "That isn't a glint you want to know about. Margaret's torque-jawed because she didn't get the promotion. She'll get over it and will probably rebound twice as strong. Don't worry about her. She's a survivor.''

Eloise wished she could say the same about herself. ''Well, keep looking at her,'' she pleaded. ''You're sure to feel a connection soon.'' Though none could be more powerful than the one she'd felt that night when she'd shot herself in the foot and lifted her gaze to meet Blake's stormy gray eyes across the room. Dear heaven, she'd never known such potent force. No matter what happened when she returned to her celestial home, the impact of that first spark of magic—and all that had followed—would be with her throughout eternity.

She sighed as Crankshank spoke again.

''I realize these treasure hunts of mine are vexatious to some of you, but I believe I have the finest management team in any company in the country.'' He nodded toward Terry and Ettienne. ''Even those of you who are easily distracted. Your enthusiasm, however misdirected, was admirable. I'm hoping Spencer, as my new Vice President of Marketing, can harness all that energy.''

''I'll do my very best, sir,'' Spencer replied.

There was a general murmuring of agreement.

Eloise's heart was far too heavy to allow her to join in the newfound harmony. She'd be leaving her earthly assignment soon. Whenever Hubert found it convenient, she assumed. And now each minute was painful as she waited for Cupid's magic potion to do its work on Blake and Margaret.

Feigning illness, she pushed her chair back from the table.

"I'm sorry," she whispered to Blake. More sorry than he would ever realize.

Swallowing a sob, she fled to her room.

Blake started to follow. He didn't know what was bothering Eloise but he wanted to help.

He glanced across the table, almost in the hope that another woman would be able to give him a clue about what had gone wrong. Instead what he saw was devastation in Margaret's eyes and shock that she hadn't won the promotion. He felt sympathy for her, and a new camaraderie, but knew he wouldn't get the insight he needed.

Unfortunately, Spencer snared him before he could leave the table. It wasn't exactly polite for Blake to walk out on his new boss. So he stayed, making small talk and worrying about what was wrong with Eloise.

Escaping at last, he went upstairs, entered his own room and ditched his ersatz suit of armor. Then he knocked softly on the connecting door between their rooms. When there was no answer, he turned the knob. The door opened easily.

At the sight of Eloise standing at the window of the darkened room, a band tightened around Blake's chest. She was so beautiful, she simply took his breath away.

Moonbeams played through her hair, giving her curls silver highlights as though they'd been sprinkled with fairy dust. Her togalike gown bared one softly sloping shoulder, revealing creamy smooth flesh that begged for his caress. Her head was bowed slightly, inviting a kiss on her nape, and she was hugging herself. Blake wanted it to be his arms that embraced her.

He crossed the room on silent feet. "Angel..."

Slowly, she lifted her head. Tears glistened on her cheeks. "Why are you here?" she whispered.

Dear Lord, he loved the tiny indentation above her upper lip, the bowed shape of her mouth, its taste. "I was worried about you." *I want to make love with you.*

"I thought you'd be with Margaret."

"Why do you keep saying things like that? I don't want to be with Margaret." With his fingertip, he wiped a tear from her cheek. "I want to be with you."

A frown stitched across her forehead. "The magic should be working by now."

"You're magic. And it's working fine." He dipped his head to touch a kiss to her lips—so warm, so sweet. Her special scent was all around him, a part of him, drugging him. He craved her as an addict would hunger for an ever more potent opiate.

She took a shuddering breath and closed her eyes for a moment. Her blond lashes rested like half-moons on her pale cheeks. "I'll be leaving soon."

"That doesn't mean we can't see each other again." Dear God, he didn't want to be away from her for a single day—or night. "Tell me your address. Your phone number. I've got some stuff to work out but as soon as I can, I'll be on the first flight—"

"It doesn't work that way."

His stomach knotted. Was she turning him down? "Please, angel, tell me—"

"I *have* told you. I'm a cupid. And I've got to go back..." Her voice caught and another tear spilled down her cheek. "I'll never forget you, Blake. Not through all the rest of eternity."

This was crazy. He didn't believe in cupids. Hell, until he'd met Eloise he hadn't even believed in love. Now anything seemed possible and she kept insisting she was leaving. He'd never see her again.

It was as though Crankshank had played the world's worst practical joke on him.

Blake gathered her into his arms. He kissed her hard and deep and long. She moaned. Or maybe it was him. He didn't know and it didn't matter. He wasn't going to let her go. Not now. Not ever.

She melted into him, her fingers kneaded into his T-shirt, and the fire that had been banked all evening built in his belly. Her mouth was soft, willing, her tongue eager to mate with his. The flames built into rippling heat throughout his body.

She shifted slightly, her arms extending around his neck, and her pelvis brushed against his hard, aching arousal. He groaned. "Oh, angel..."

The fire, the need, was going to consume him. He moved against her, half afraid she'd pull away but needing that intimate caress again. He shouldn't have worried. She stayed and nestled into the juncture of his hips, into his heat. She fit there perfectly.

"Angel, I want..."

"Yes." Her breath was a heated caress across his lips. "For as long as I'm allowed to stay."

In a quick, sure movement, she released the pin at her shoulder that held her dress. Silken fabric shimmered downward with a sibilant sound, pooling at her feet; golden moonlight gilded her naked body, revealing a narrow waist and breasts so perfect Blake thought he had died and gone to heaven.

My God! If he'd known during dinner she wasn't wearing anything beneath that dress—

He knelt, worshiping her body with his kisses.

"Blake, I—" She speared her fingers through his hair, pulling him closer. Her breathing came in sharp little pants. "I can't—"

"You taste so good. Nectar meant for the gods."

On a sudden cry, she shouted, "Blake!" He felt her trembling climax, tasted it. "Angel..."

He held her while her breathing slowed. Then he stood and carried her to the bed and laid her on the soft mattress beneath the frilly canopy. Shedding his clothes, he joined her there, bringing their bodies together until they were one. And he loved her as he had never loved any other woman before. Thoroughly. Until exhaustion set in and he had only enough strength left to hold her in his arms.

When he awoke she was gone.

10

"ELOISE!"

He bellowed her name. His feet were tangled in the bedding and he wrenched himself free, nearly falling to the floor in the process. Morning sun streamed in the windows.

She traveled on sunbeams!

Fear gripped him in a painful vise. That thought was crazy. Eloise wasn't a—

He yanked open the door to her bathroom. Modesty be damned! After what they'd done last night...

But she wasn't there.

He whirled. Maybe she'd gone downstairs for breakfast. After their energetic night, any woman would be hungry. And he'd been sleeping the sleep of the dead. Little wonder he hadn't heard her get up, hadn't heard her leave.

The indentation where her head had rested on the pillow was still there; the heavenly scent of her still filled the room. He was panicking about nothing, he told himself. She couldn't have been gone long.

He scooped up the pair of pants he'd dropped on the floor last night and tugged them on. There was no sign of Eloise's gown. She must have——

Without worrying about a shirt or shoes, he raced downstairs.

Spencer was in the dining room, adding to the selection of breakfast rolls that already filled his plate.

"Good morning," he said brightly. "Beautiful day, isn't it?"

"Have you seen Eloise?"

"No. Not yet. The first ferry to the mainland is delayed, so everyone is sleeping late. I assumed—"

"She's not upstairs."

"Have you checked outside? It's a lovely day for a stroll."

Relief, so sharp it was painful, whipped through Blake. He should have thought of that.

"Oddly enough, however," Spencer continued thoughtfully, "Hubert's among the missing, as well. Breakfast was set out—rolls and juice and coffee— but I haven't been able to locate him."

Why would Eloise have gone off with the butler? Except Blake had sensed there was some odd connection between them. "He must have taken the early ferry back."

"No. As I said, they're running late this morning. Something about an engine overhaul. The first ferry is due at noon. We'll all be going back then."

But not Hubert. Or Eloise.

Blake's spirits sank. Dear heaven, she couldn't have been telling him the truth. No way could she be a cupid. And yet, people didn't simply vanish.

Damn, if only she'd left him a note.

"Good morning, gentlemen."

For an instant, Blake thought Eloise had joined them in the dining room. Instead the female voice belonged to Margaret, who looked polished and poised in tailored slacks and a matching salmon-red jacket. Already he missed Eloise's slightly disheveled appearance and her uninhibited zest for life.

Margaret eyed Blake's state of undress with a raised brow but made no comment. "Where is everyone?" she asked instead.

"For the most part, they're sleeping late," Spencer told her.

"Eloise is gone," Blake said morosely. She wasn't anywhere on the island, or in a place where he could go to her. He knew because there was an empty place in his heart that he feared might never be filled.

Picking up a china cup and saucer from the sideboard, Margaret poured herself some coffee. "Eloise left without you?"

"She told me she had to go." He hadn't believed her. Damn, how could he have been so stupid? If he'd only listened when she'd tried to tell him.

"I don't know how she could have gotten off the island," Spencer said.

"On a sunbeam," Blake muttered, still not fully convinced that what his gut was telling him was actually true.

Margaret placed her hand lightly on his arm. "She'll be back. I saw the way she looked at you…" She cleared her throat as though a lump of emotion had formed. "I envy you both."

"She's a very special lady," Blake agreed. The

first ever female apprentice cupid. She'd wanted so much to succeed in her assignment. Dear God, did he actually believe…

Margaret's cup rattled slightly against the saucer as she placed it on the table. "Last night, watching the two of you together, I realized… There's a man who looks at me that way. I've been putting him off. My parents disapprove, you see. But now…"

"You're in love," Spencer said, and it wasn't a question. The quiet smile on Margaret's face, softer than usual, and more genuine, gave her away.

"The truth is, I'm glad you got the promotion, Spencer. I think it's time I devote a little more energy to my personal life and less to the company. And less to pleasing my parents," she added with a melancholy twist of her lips.

"I hope you won't be leaving Crest all together," Spencer said. "You'd be a very difficult person to replace."

The surprisingly soft, gentle side of Margaret vanished and her tough exterior reappeared as quickly as if she'd changed masks. "Not a chance. I still plan to outsell and outdeal every other regional director in the country. You'd better warn them, Spencer. This time next year, I expect to be top dog."

Blake believed she'd do it, too. Among other factors, his enthusiasm for the job was at rock bottom and normally he was her biggest competitor. Now his heart simply wasn't in playing the game.

"Sugar, they sure must have squeezed the living daylights out of you at that ol' marketing retreat."

Blake's secretary sauntered into his office, her hips swaying. "You haven't done a lick of work since you've been back, and it's been two weeks."

"Don't remind me," he mumbled. The stack of file folders on his desk had risen to avalanche proportions. He couldn't seem to concentrate. He wanted to punch someone. He wanted to climb on top of the nearest skyscraper and scream, Come back, Eloise!

God, he was really losing it.

"If I didn't know better, I'd say Cupid had stung you a good one with his arrow."

Startled, he studied Paula for a moment. "Why would you say that?" How would she know? Did women have a second sense about matters of love that men didn't possess?

"It's simple enough to see." Lifting her hip, she sat on the edge of his desk. Her skirt hiked up a little too high on her thigh but Blake wasn't moved. He didn't think Paula intended him to be. And the only leg that would turn him on these days belonged to Eloise Periwinkle.

"You spend half the day looking out the window," she explained. "And you've been losing weight, which means you're not eating right. Not to mention, for the first time since I've worked here, you aren't cracking the whip over your team. I'd say that adds up to a serious romantic entanglement."

He sighed. "You don't know the half of it." Blake wasn't sure he could explain it himself. He'd only known Eloise for three days. Now she was his life.

Fortunately, his big concern about Stevie had been resolved. Apparently Spencer had mentioned to Crankshank that something was worrying Blake. The next thing he knew, Crest Enterprises was picking up the hospital tab and covering the cost of therapy. Blake somehow suspected Spencer had skipped the bonus that went with his promotion, passing on the money to cover Stevie's expenses.

Hell of a good boss, Blake thought.

"So what are you going to do about being in love?" Paula asked.

"I don't know." He wished to heaven he did.

Her eyes narrowed. "You did remember to tell the little lady how you feel."

Had he? Surely he'd mentioned his feelings. But maybe she hadn't believed him. It had all happened so fast.

No, that wasn't quite right. He'd said that he loved her. The problem was, at the time he hadn't really believed it himself.

Now he did.

"Men!" Paula huffed. Standing, she paced in long-legged strides across the room to stand by the window. "Do you men really expect us to read your minds?"

"We didn't really have much time together," he said, defending his oversight. His stupidity. He should have made his feelings abundantly clear. Closed the deal right then and there with no loose ends. No escape clause. "I would have gotten around—"

"Do it now."

"I can't. I don't know where she is."

Paula threw up her hands in dismay. "So try looking in the telephone directory."

"She doesn't exactly live nearby."

"Try e-mail. Online romance is the big thing these days."

"I don't think that would work with Eloise. I doubt she has a computer."

"Well, for heaven's sake, sugar, figure it out for yourself. You're in the sign business, aren't you? Don't we have a motto that says With The Right Sign You Can Reach The World?"

"In this case it would take a hell of a big sign." How many watts of power would it take to build a sign that could be seen in the heavens? Assuming that's where Eloise was.

"Well, do something, boss, and do it soon. This having nothing to do is driving me crazy."

"You could rearrange the files. I can never find what I'm looking for."

She gave him a look that spoke volumes about how much he had insulted her. "I'll have you know, the files are in perfect order."

"Then tell me this, Paula. Why the hell is Snappy Pizza filed under H-to-L?"

"The answer is obvious." She drew herself up to her full five-foot-ten. "You go to Snappy Pizza when you're *hungry.*"

"Hungry?" he echoed, confused.

"Which begins with an *H.*" With that, she turned and marched out of the room.

A logical answer in a bizarre sort of way, he decided. Using the same twisted logic, maybe he should build a sign that Eloise could see—or hear about— wherever she was. A sign that would tell her how much he loved her.

He swiveled his chair around to look out the window at the Atlanta skyline. It would have to be the biggest, most spectacular electronic billboard Crest Enterprises had ever built.

If he could convince Eloise to come back to him, it would be worth every penny he spent.

ELOISE HAD EXPECTED to be called onto the celestial carpet for her failure as an apprentice cupid. She hadn't expected to face Hubert's boss's boss, the Celestial Senior Manager of Human Relations.

Dejected, she stood on the silver-lined carpet of clouds in front of Montgomery Upright's desk and studied the tips of her sandals. It didn't really matter what happened to her now. Without Blake, she only existed from one timeless moment to the next. She'd left her heart, her very soul, with him on earth.

"Your case is most unusual, Ms. Periwinkle."

"Yes, sir." She imagined few in celestial history had messed up as often as she had.

Mr. Upright was a tall man, with smooth features, kind blue eyes and a patient smile. "In all of your assignments, you have demonstrated amazing ingenuity in your determination to succeed, sometimes under difficult circumstances."

She did a mental double take. "I have?"

He nodded sagely. "Not many guardian angels would have been able to think as fast on their feet as you did. Saving two lives, when you'd been assigned to rescue only one poor soul, was quite admirable."

"I don't think the mayor was all that pleased at the time with his impromptu swim."

"Perhaps not." He chuckled softly.

Eloise began to relax a little. Mr. Upright was such a kind man, maybe her punishment wouldn't be too awful after all.

"And then there was that, uh, unusual incident while you were assigned to the Baby Department."

Heat flushed her cheeks. There was no way she could explain that transgression away. She'd never regret it, either, she thought stubbornly. That forgotten little boy needed a home and—

"I'd say you found an ingenious solution to a difficult problem."

She swallowed hard. "I hope the little boy is happy."

"When I last checked, he was quite content." Pausing, Upright rearranged one of the files on his desk. "This most recent episode demonstrates again your…shall we say, unique talents."

Now she was going to get it, but good. Not only hadn't Margaret and Blake fallen in love, due to her failed assignment, but Eloise *had*. Yet there could be no worse punishment than having lost Blake.

Her gaze lowered. "I'm sorry," she whispered, the apology thick in her throat.

"You needn't be. You were operating under a severe handicap, which none of us recognized until it was too late.''

Her head came up. ''I was?''

''It seems Hubert was far more inflexible about his departmental staffing requirements than we had realized. He intended that you fail, Ms. Periwinkle. Your efforts in the face of the obstacles he placed before you were commendable.''

Eloise wished there was a chair nearby. Her knees had gone weak with relief, and the knot in her stomach had suddenly eased.

As if he could read her mind, Mr. Upright stood and rolled his chair around to her side of his desk. Taking her elbow, he seated her.

''It was Hubert, I'm afraid, who locked you and Mr. Donovan in the ballroom together.''

The memory of Blake's kiss that day was so sharp, her hand rose to cover her lips. ''Why...why did Hubert do that?''

''He assumed you would be unable to carry out your assignment if he kept Mr. Donovan separated from Ms. Wykowski. That was the reason he locked you in the lookout room all night, as well.'' Mr. Upright patted her hand gently. ''I'm not sure he fully anticipated the repercussions of his unauthorized actions.''

Her cheeks flamed. She remembered exactly what those repercussions had been—in exquisite, unforgettable detail. Evidently Mr. Upright had a fair idea of what had happened, too.

''If it is any consolation, Hubert has been severely

reprimanded and demoted to a position of far less authority. He won't impede our future plans for Cupid's Celestial Division. In fact, I expect there'll be a complete overhaul of that department in the very near future.''

''Besides trying to keep Blake away from Margaret, did he do anything else that—''

''The original potion he gave you was severely diluted, about ten percent as powerful as it should have been. It would be most unusual for humans to fall in love, given such a small dose.''

''But Blake did,'' she protested vehemently. ''But not with the right woman. Because I…I shot myself in the foot and…'' How could she admit, even now, that she'd fallen in love, too? Surely that was so far beyond the limits of celestial protocol as to be totally unacceptable, even in the eyes of a kind man like Mr. Upright.

''Perhaps he did fall in love with the right woman,'' he said softly.

She looked at him blankly. ''I don't understand.''

''All of this, uh, unusual activity surrounding your case caused me to retrieve your file from our archives, Ms. Periwinkle.'' He picked up a folder that was nearly five inches thick, then rested his hip on the edge of his desk as he opened it.

Oh, boy, now he'd know she'd flunked harp lessons, too.

''It took my staff quite some time to sort out all the facts, but it appears there has been a bureaucratic error. A serious one. It appears you don't actually belong here.''

Oh, hell!

His eyebrows shot up. He cleared his throat. "For reasons that are not entirely clear, when you were in the Baby Department—"

"You said what I did with the little boy wasn't all that bad.'' Dear heaven, she hadn't expected her punishment would send her to—

"No, no. You misunderstand. When you, yourself, were an infant waiting for a family, something went wrong. There should have been a family available. You reached the top of the list and simply… Apparently your name was inadvertently deleted from among those waiting.''

"That's why I was never chosen?'' she asked, stunned by his revelation. "I always thought…I blamed myself.'' She'd been so sure there was something wrong with her since no family had chosen her. She'd also never felt entirely comfortable among those who moved with such serenity in her celestial home. She didn't belong. Anywhere. And now Mr. Upright was telling her that it wasn't her fault. They'd made a mistake.

"It was our error, Eloise. And we regret it enormously. I trust you will accept our apologies.''

"Oh, sure.'' She shrugged and smiled weakly. But what did that mean now? She wasn't about to become an overnight success as a harp player. No talent there. So where in the world *did* she belong?

"We thought you might like to return to earth.''

She nearly fell out of the chair. "Ear...th?" Her voice cracked. *Oh, please, please, please.*

"This time as a mortal," he added. His smile was as kind and understanding as any she'd ever seen. In a fatherly gesture, he extended his hand. "There's something I'd like you to see."

She went with him willingly enough, though she couldn't imagine what he had in mind. Meanwhile, her mind was back on earth with Blake, remembering every *mortal* moment they'd spent together on Crankshank Island.

An odd thought popped into her head. "Mr. Upright, when Blake was trying to get the flag down for his first clue, the padlock popped open. I was wondering..." If she didn't belong up here, how could she have possibly created a miracle, even a small one.

"Have you considered you might have your own guardian angel, one who has been working overtime of late?" His smile was just the slightest bit smug and she wondered...

"No, I hadn't thought about that," she said, curious. Could he have been...

He cleared his throat. "A good manager needs to stay current with his operations."

Oh, my heavens! She'd had the super big boss watching out for her.

They'd reached the large bank of clouds that marked the edge of the celestial limits, and Mr. Upright stopped.

She peered down—way, way down—and squinted. It was dark down there. Nighttime.

"My heaven sakes!" A huge electronic billboard blinked rhythmically, the colors rippling red, green and blue. The sign was so large, it must have filled an entire baseball stadium. Well, a small stadium, at any rate.

But it was the words that made her heart tumble.

Eloise, I Love You. Please Come Back.

Her chin trembled and she bit her lower lip. Tears pooled in her eyes, creating prisms of color. *Dear, sweet Blake*. He did love her. It wasn't just the magic potion; that would have worn off by now.

Mr. Upright's hand rested on her shoulder. "It's your choice, Eloise. You may go, or stay here with us."

Her decision took no thought at all. "I want to go back. Oh, yes, please. May I?" Standing, she searched the horizon for a likely looking moonbeam. Fortunately the moon was full and there were plenty to choose from. Then a thought struck her. "Not that I'm ungrateful, or don't like it here, but..."

The laughter of the head of Human Relations rumbled across the clouds like a miniature thunderstorm. "Go with our best wishes. But remember—"

She glanced up at him.

"We'll be expecting you back here in seventy earth years or so. You might want to take a few harp lessons while you're there. You'll be needing them."

She grinned. "Yes, sir. I'll do that." It might take her that long to get the knack of the instrument.

Turning, she ran for the edge, then suddenly dug

her heels in. Bits and pieces of clouds sprayed into
the air.

"What's wrong?" Mr. Upright asked.

"Before I go... It'll just take me a minute." Leaving the super-senior head of Human Relations standing there looking dumbfounded, she raced away. She
hoped Blake would approve of her idea.

In no time she was back again, slightly breathless
with both excitement and anticipation.

"Is everything all right?" Mr. Upright asked. He
tilted his head slightly, as though he wasn't quite sure
he should set her loose on her own.

"Yes, sir. Everything's fine now." With that, she
leaped over the edge of the cloud before Upright
could ask her any more questions, grabbed herself a
sturdy moonbeam, and slid toward earth and the man
she loved.

11

THE HELICOPTERS were gone.

They'd been hovering around the Little League baseball field for days, photographers snapping pictures, news cameras rolling tape of Blake's electronic billboard, reporters interviewing him. The news had made all the major networks, every metropolitan newspaper in the country and the wire service had carried the story to Europe.

The publicity had made Crest Enterprises so famous, Crankshank was thinking about opening an overseas division. Eager to test gourmet cooking in France, Spencer was considering heading the new division. That would leave the stateside job of Vice President of Marketing open for Blake.

He hadn't given it much thought.

Everyone had been waiting for Eloise to show up. If she were anywhere on earth, she would have heard about the billboard flashing his confession of love.

But she hadn't come and the front-page stories had shifted to a new international crisis and the next human-interest story.

Blake's mother and sister had thought he was crazy; his nephew Steve thought the whole idea of falling in love was yucky. But his entire family had been in the stands waiting with him those first few nights, his nephew still on crutches.

Now Blake was the only one waiting in the bleachers. But soon he'd have to pull the plug on his scheme. The neighbors had complained about the noise and bright lights. The billboard was on a timer. In five minutes it would go dark.

Failure didn't come easily to him. It never had.

He checked his watch. The glowing dial indicated only a few minutes had passed since he'd looked at it last. Time had never moved so slowly as it had this past month, since he'd last seen Eloise.

Since he'd *lost* Eloise.

Leaning back, he rested his elbows on the bleacher bench behind him and gazed up at a skyful of stars.

His eyes narrowed, focusing on a white form catapulting toward earth.

A UFO? A comet? A falling star? He couldn't make it out.

Thinking it was probably nothing more than a weather balloon that had escaped its mooring, he shook his head, sighed and closed his eyes.

That's when she slammed into him.

The breath was driven from his lungs in a whoosh.

"Oops!"

"Eloise?" He coughed. His ribs vibrated with the bruising shot they'd taken, like getting tackled by a three-hundred-pound linebacker.

"Oh, dear. I must have misjudged my speed. Did I hurt you?"

"No. I'm fine." He coughed again, still trying to regain his breath. "Perfect, in fact. Never better." She was straddling him and he wrapped his arms around her. This time he damn well wasn't ever going to let go. "You're back!"

"Mr. Upright said I could come. He's the super big boss—much higher than Hubert—and he told me there'd been this terrible mistake. Hubert, by the way, is in big trouble. He really shouldn't have interfered but I'm so glad he did." She kissed Blake and it was like tasting a bit of heaven. "I wouldn't have gotten to come back if he hadn't."

None of what she was saying made sense. Frankly, Blake didn't care about Hubert or this Mr. Upright person. "Eloise, I love you."

She grinned. "I know. I saw your sign." She kissed him again. "That was so sweet of you."

The way she was straddling him was doing a number on his libido. Her silver-blond hair was a tumble of mussed curls, as if she'd just had great sex. Which is exactly what Blake wanted to do with her. But he had to get some things straightened out before he could worry about that.

"Eloise, do you love me?"

"Of course I do." Her eyes widened, reflecting the vibrant colors of the electronic sign. "And it's not just the magic potion, either. I would have loved you no matter where or how we'd met. We were meant for each other."

Sweet, hot relief surged through Blake as the lights on the billboard switched off. It didn't matter now.

He had Eloise exactly where he wanted her—in his arms. "I don't deserve you, angel."

"Of course you do. You must have done something really wonderful or Cupid's department wouldn't have assigned me to help you fall in love."

"Then I'm the luckiest man in the world that you did such a really good job."

"Thank you." She giggled a little, a sound like tiny bells ringing on a cold night. "Most of the time my projects don't work out quite this well."

"Marry me."

She went very still. For a moment Blake thought she might refuse him.

"Yes, Blake Donovan," she whispered. Her beautifully shaped lips trembled. In the moonlight he saw tears sheening her eyes. "Nothing in the universe would make me happier than to marry you."

"Thank heaven." He exhaled the breath he'd been holding.

"Yes, that too."

"I want it to be soon. Unless you want to wait awhile," he hedged. "I admit we haven't known each other long."

"The sooner the better as far as I'm concerned. But there is one little thing…"

He eyed her suspiciously. "What little thing?"

"Well, two little things, actually."

"Yes?"

"I'd like to take harp lessons."

He shrugged. How awful could that be? Everyone needed a hobby. "Fine by me. What else?"

"Well, before I left, I stopped by the Baby Department..."

My God, was she pregnant? Not that he'd mind the prospect of her having his baby. Lots of them. But he'd been a fool not to use protection, for both their sakes.

"I found a little boy that would be perfect for us," she said. "He's got beautiful stormy gray eyes just like yours and the prettiest smile. And he wants a family. I'd hate to see him forgotten or thinking no one wanted him. So I thought maybe..."

"Angel, whenever you want to start a family is fine by me." He pulled her closer and she snuggled into his embrace. Nuzzling her tousled hair, he inhaled deeply of her heavenly scent.

"He's going to grow up and do wonderful things. He'll be an astronomer."

"Maybe we ought to get him into kindergarten first before we make too many plans for him."

"No, you'll see. He's going to be a really important person." She sighed. "I think he's going to want to have a puppy, too."

"Terrific," he murmured.

"I know just the kind he'll like. Sort of a mixed—"

"Whatever you say, sweetheart. I only want you to make me one promise."

"What's that?"

"That you won't go flying around on moonbeams anymore. I don't want you landing in some other guy's lap. You're too much of a temptation to resist."

She sighed and turned so they could both look up at the night sky, so filled with stars now that the billboard had switched off it looked as if they might burst from the heavens. "I promise."

Eloise grinned. Luckily he hadn't said a thing about not sliding down banisters.

Sexy, desirable and...a daddy?

THE AUSTRALIANS

Stories of romance Australian-style, guaranteed to fulfill that sense of adventure!

This February 1999 look for

Baby Down Under

by Ann Charlton

Riley Templeton was a hotshot Queensland lawyer with a reputation for ruthlessness and a weakness for curvaceous blondes. Alexandra Page was everything that Riley *wasn't* looking for in a woman, but when she finds a baby on her doorstep that leads her to the dashing lawyer, he begins to see the virtues of brunettes—and babies!

The Wonder from Down Under: where spirited women win the hearts of Australia's most independent men!

Available February 1999
at your favorite retail outlet.

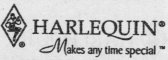

HARLEQUIN®
Makes any time special ™

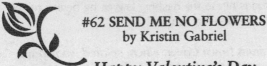
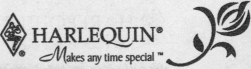

MEN at WORK

All work and no play?
Not these men!

January 1999
SOMETHING WORTH KEEPING by Kathleen Eagle
He worked with iron and steel, and was as wild as the mustangs that were his passion. She was a high-class horse trainer from the East. Was her gentle touch enough to tame his unruly heart?

February 1999
HANDSOME DEVIL by Joan Hohl
His roguish good looks and intelligence drew women like magnets, but Luke Branson was having too much fun to marry again. Then Selena McInnes strolled before him and turned his life upside down!

March 1999
STARK LIGHTNING by Elaine Barbieri
The boss's daughter was ornery, stubborn and off-limits for cowboy Branch Walker! But Valentine was also nearly impossible to resist. Could they negotiate a truce...or a surrender?

Available at your favorite retail outlet!

MEN AT WORK™

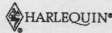 

Look us up on-line at: http://www.romance.net

PMAW4

LOVE & LAUGH

INTO MARCH!

#63 FROM HERE TO MATERNITY
Right Stork, Wrong Address
Cheryl Anne Porter
Murphy Brown meets June Cleaver? Up-and-coming ad
exec Laura Sloan loves her single, child-free life just the
way it is. So what's she going to do when she finds an
adorable, *abandoned* baby boy in her office *and* her first
love, gorgeous Grant Maguire, on her doorstep? Suddenly
she's got two males to contend with—and she hasn't a
clue what to do with either of them. But Grant's kisses are
making her think it's time she found out....

#64 HIS BODYGUARD
Lois Greiman
Nathan Fox doesn't want a bodyguard, but after the last
threat on his life he needs one. Luck is on his side when
one Brittany O'Shay, petite, curvy and beautiful, applies.
He hires her, hoping she'll be more interested in exploring
his body than actually guarding it, leaving him free to
figure out who wanted to harm him. Little does Nathan
know that this is one woman who takes her job seriously...
all business and no play. And how he'd like to play....

Chuckles available now:

#61 COURTING CUPID
Charlotte Maclay
#62 SEND ME NO FLOWERS
Kristin Gabriel

LOVE & LAUGHTER™